DOG TAGS

BOOK FOUR
DIVIDED
WE FALL

C. ALEXANDER LONDON

SCHOLASTIC INC.

ISBN 978-0-545-47707-9

10 9 8 7 6 5 4 3 2   13 14 15 16 17

Printed in the U.S.A.   40
First printing, April 2013

For the next generation of peacemakers, that they may do better than those who have come before.

"Human beings can be awful cruel to one another."
— Mark Twain, *The Adventures of Huckleberry Finn*

CHAPTER 1

MANHUNT

Hunting down a man ain't like hunting down a raccoon. Raccoons are smart and quick. They move like summer lightning. They hide up trees or deep down in burrows, where you gotta smoke 'em out. Men don't hide half so well as raccoons, and there weren't ever one born that could hide from Dash. He was the best hound dog in the whole state of Mississippi, and he was gonna prove it that morning in the summer of 1863.

A piece of gray cloth had snagged on a willow branch. I pulled it down so that Dash could sniff it and catch the scent of the man we hunted. He wagged his tail and his big jowls dripped with slobber.

"Go get 'im, boy!" I said, and Dash took off, barking and running to beat the devil.

One thing I knew for sure was that if I was on the run, I wouldn't go leaving bits of my uniform snagged on branches for a hound dog like Dash to smell. The way I figured it, the man we were after was as good as caught.

Dash was on the chase. I ran behind.

The air hung wet and heavy, so my shirt was all stuck to me, and I wanted to tear it off and dive into a cool pond for a swim more than I wanted to chase through the woods, getting bit by critters and slapped in the face by stinging branches, but I had my sworn duty to do, and the cowardly rascal we was after weren't gonna give me and Dash the slip.

I couldn't imagine what would make a yella-bellied coward desert the great Confederate Army, fighting to protect our land from the Yanks' tyranny, but he'd have to be some kind of fool to run off and come all the way back here. We didn't give army deserters no quarter, not in Meridian, Mississippi.

My big brother, Julius, always said that Washington, DC'd burn to the ground before the good folks of Meridian gave up the cause of freedom. We were the heart of the Confederacy, as Julius said it. Julius may've been just sixteen years old, four more than me, but the Confederacy needed men, so Julius lied about his age so he could fight for the Southern cause and for our way of life.

Also, they paid a fifty-dollar bounty for enlisting . . . but we hadn't seen that money yet.

We didn't have no slaves because Pa didn't approve and we couldn't afford one even so, but Pa weren't no abolitionist neither. As Pa would put it, we weren't fighting for slavery. We were fighting against tyranny.

Abolitionists wanted to outlaw slavery in the whole country and let free all the slaves there was. They didn't have no plan what to do with all them folks after they was free, and the way I saw it, that was a problem right there. There weren't enough work for folks like my Pa as it was. You add thousands of freed slaves looking for wages to the mix, and, well, it wouldn't do, says Pa. But that's just what the Yankees wanted, and that's why Mississippi was the second state to stand up and secede from the Union. That's what the war was all about. As Pa would say, we were fightin' for Freedom, Justice, Honor, and the Great State of Mississippi.

Pa said that if the South was gonna change its peculiar ways, then the South had to do it on its own and no Billy Yank from Chicago or Boston could force that change on us. Our way of life suited us just fine, and we weren't forcing it on anyone else, so why should they wage war to force their way of life on us? I figured the slaves might say different, but folks said they was happier with the way things were too, and that weren't really a concern of mine. I just wanted to do my part, like my brother.

My parents were hoppin' mad when Julius came home saying how he was off to fight, on account of him telling lies about his age and not asking Pa permission first and such, but Julius is a real smooth talker and he said "Freedom, Justice, Honor, and the Great State of Mississippi" right back to my father and, well, Pa couldn't argue with that. He'd put those ideas into Julius's head in the first place. You can't plant wheat in the ground and get mad when wheat grows from the seeds.

So we said good-bye, and he's been gone a while now. I was jealous that Julius got to go be heroic when I had to stay home and look after the house and get educated and do my chores and such. I wanted to fight against tyranny too. But Julius told me I better look after his dog, Dash, while he was gone, and that's what I did, because I figured we all find different ways to serve.

It didn't take long for me and Dash to find a job. Like I said, he's the best coonhound there is, and the Home Guard came knockin' on our door to see if we might want to use his nose to help them out. Northern spies were abroad in the countryside, and so were runaway slaves and deserters. The Home Guard was supposed to catch 'em. They said a dog like Dash'd sure come in handy for that.

I wanted to do it right away, but Pa didn't approve of that either. I won out because I learned to argue just like Julius, and the Home Guard got me doing patrols with them and chasing down no-good deserters. I couldn't wait to catch one and give him what for.

So instead of swimming in the pond or lazing about the afternoon, I ran.

Dash jumped over a fallen tree, barking and snarling, then he turned a sharp left and skittered to a stop. His nose worked the ground, his big floppy ears swooshing back and forth as his head swiveled from side to side. I heard Winslow and them others from the Home Guard huffing along way behind us. They couldn't keep up, which was fine with me. I wanted to catch the coward we was after by myself.

"Slow down, Dash, I only got two legs to your four!" I told my dog.

Dash didn't slow down. He barreled through the brush to the edge of a field and slid right under the wooden posts.

I had to climb over the fence, and I tore my trousers in doing it. I knew Ma would be upset about that, as I don't have enough clothes to go ripping up the ones I was wearing, but I kept running because catching this deserter was more important than torn trousers.

I recognized we were on the edge of Widow Parker's farm, and I felt real sorry stomping through her fields like I was, just before harvest time too, but there was nothing to be done for it. I ran across with Dash, and then we found the railroad tracks on the other side of the field. A small lineman's cabin sat beside the track, leaning heavily like the building itself was getting ready to lie down for a nap, and Dash ran right to it, jumping at the door and barking and slamming his big brown paws on the wood so hard, I thought for sure the building would topple.

He circled and barked and wouldn't budge no farther than that squat little shack.

"He in there, boy?" I asked, my heart pounding in my chest. I couldn't hardly contain my smile. I was about to catch my first criminal. "Okay, now!" I shouted. "You been caught fair and square. You come out now and surrender!"

The only answer I got was a warm breeze over the fields, the rustle of grass, and the creak of old wood. I stepped closer to the door of the cabin. It was loose on the leather straps that held it closed. Through the slit of the door where it hung open, I saw nothing but blackness inside. The sun shined right down on us overheard, bright white hot, but I felt a chill go through me.

I'd never seen a deserter before, but I figured they were cowards. Anyone who'd run from the army had to be a coward, but I never thought before how sometimes it was cowards who was the most dangerous of all. A trapped animal is the one that bites you.

I should've waited for Winslow and the others, but Julius was off someplace fighting the Yanks, and what would he think of his little brother being scared of one lone deserter hiding in a lineman's cabin? If Julius could take to the field of battle for the honor and glory of Mississippi, then I could sure enough capture the coward hiding in the cabin.

I stepped up and pushed the door open with my toe.

"Come on out now!" I yelled, but my voice cracked real high. It was always doin' that at the worst possible times, and I looked around real quick to make sure Winslow and the others wasn't around to hear it.

Inside the cabin, it was silent as a tomb. Afternoon light slashed into the dim space. Dust danced in the light, but the cabin looked empty. It was no bigger than a pantry, and I didn't see anyplace for the deserter to hide himself. For a moment, I thought maybe Dash had caught the wrong scent, but Dash never did lead me wrong on a hunt before. Why would he start now, when it was so important?

I stepped inside the cabin. "Come on out!" I repeated. Dash whined, and I heard him circling the cabin on the outside. He weren't allowed inside back at home, and I guess he figured the rules was the same out here. I sure would have felt better if he followed me in, though.

The air was even heavier in that little cabin, and it smelled sour, like sweat and tobacco and turned meat. I wrinkled my nose. I couldn't imagine a man choosing to hide here, no matter how afraid he was of being brought to justice. I wanted to turn and step right back out into the sunlight and the fresh air, and I was just about to do so when a hand clamped over my face and a heavy arm yanked me back.

"Don't you move, or I'll snap your neck," a man commanded as he pulled me off my feet and kicked the cabin door shut, with Dash still outside.

CHAPTER 2

CAUGHT

Dash barked, and I heard his paws scraping the wood of the door. It shuddered, and I prayed the whole place would come crashing down around us so I could escape, but the walls held.

"Call off your dog!" the man commanded me. "Quiet him down."

I felt the scratchy wool of his army uniform damp against my neck. His breath reeked of tobacco. His hand relaxed on my face so I could move my mouth. I wanted to scream but knew he'd kill me before any help could come to get me. I felt like a fool for falling into his trap, but I'd done it, and the best I could do now was obey him and hope he let me go.

"Dash, hush!" I ordered, and Dash fell silent outside.

I worried that Winslow and the others wouldn't be able to find me at all. This deserter would just kill me and Dash and run off to hide someplace else. He'd get away with desertion and now with murder. I tried to twist around to see if he looked like a murderer. His grip was too tight, and I couldn't turn to see him. I couldn't figure what a murderer was supposed to look like anyhow, so I stopped struggling.

"Mister," I said. "Why don't you just let me go? I promise I won't tell where you're hid."

I wasn't used to lying, because Pa always said liars are just another kind of coward, and a brave man has nothing to fear from the truth, but I figured when a coward's got you by the throat, sometimes you *have* to lie.

"What's your name, boy?" the man snarled.

"Andrew," I choked out. "Andrew Burford."

"Why are you chasing me?" the man demanded.

"I'm just out hunting with my dog," I said, lying some more. Lies are like bees. They don't come just one at a time. You start messing with 'em and they swarm. Sometimes, I guess, they sting.

"Hunting?" the man snorted. "Where's your rifle?"

"I —" He had me there. I didn't think my lie through real clearly. I didn't have anything like a weapon at all, except Dash.

"You're with the Home Guard," the man said. "Bunch of criminals and cutthroats, you lot are."

"Don't you go insulting them," I snapped right back at him. "The Home Guard keeps folks safe. We do our part, like real men! Real men don't run off like you done."

"What do you know about real men?" The man's hand gripped my arm like a vise. It hurt, but I didn't flinch. I didn't want him to know it hurt. "You seen the elephant, boy?"

I shook my head. The man was crazed. What was he talking about elephants for?

The man laughed his toothy, yellow laugh. "That's what they call the battle, you know. Seein' the elephant. Ha-ha! I seen the elephant. I rode the elephant like a Persian king! Until you seen the elephant, you have no idea what kind of man you are. War ain't like in books. Real men? *Ha!*"

I squirmed, but he held me tight. It was so dark in that little cabin, I couldn't see much but my feet dangling in the air. On the ground below 'em, I saw the man's feet, bare beneath the gray trousers of his tattered army uniform. One of them looked all swollen and full of pus, and I imagined it was mighty painful to him. I was glad. I wanted the man to be hurting.

"You're a criminal," I told him. "And you're gonna face justice!"

"I'm a farmer," the man said. "I got a mother at home, just south of Jackson, and I come back for the harvest. That's all."

"General Grant already took Jackson," I said. "You'd be a fool to go that way. Union soldiers all over it."

The man snorted loud through his nose. "No matter. My mother can't do the harvest alone, and she'll starve if we don't get the crops in. Yanks ain't gonna help her, and we don't have nobody to do our work for us. Not like these rich generals, who can keep their farms running with slaves while they keep us fighting and dying for 'em. No, sir. Their slaves live better than we do, you know that? I'm through with it, hear me? I ain't dying and I ain't killing for no rich man anymore. I done things on their account that'd make a grave robber chilled to the bone. I ain't doin' no more."

"You swore an oath when you joined up," I said. "Just like my brother swore an oath. Only cowards go breaking their oaths just 'cause they afraid. Have you no honor?"

The man laughed a raspy laugh. He spat a phlegmy wad onto the hard-packed earth floor of the cabin. "Big words for such a little runt. I bet your brother's out there swearing new oaths of his own in the battle . . . if he ain't crying and wet-ting himself when the Yank guns start blazing."

"My brother ain't like you!" I yelled, and wiggled down to stomp his bare foot with my shoe just as hard as I could.

"Gah!" he yelled, and doubled over, dropping me to the ground. I hit the earth hard and threw myself at the door. From the corner of my eye, I saw the flash of a knife blade as I pushed the door open with my fingertips. The deserter slashed at me. I felt the sting on my back as the knife sliced my skin, but the man didn't stab it in.

He didn't have the chance.

In a roar of fur and teeth and claws, Dash came leaping through the open door, lit up by the sun behind him. His big ears spread out like the wings of a hawk, and the dog crashed right on top of the no-good deserter, knocking him to the ground. The man lost his grip on the knife and it fell to the dirt, still wet with my blood.

"Ah!" he screamed. Dash bit into the man's shoulder, just south of his neck, and then the dog yanked his head from side to side, and I swear, Dash would have torn the man's head from his neck if I hadn't told him to stop.

Dash growled, his floppy lips wobbling against the man's skin. He didn't let go, and the man moved to shove him off.

"Don't you do that, mister," I said, "or I'll tell Dash to rip you apart. You just lie still."

The man groaned but let his arms fall down his sides. He looked up at the ceiling of the cabin, and he was on his back right in the shaft of light through the door, and it was the first time I got a good look at his face.

He had red hair and a scraggly red beard and a big scar running down his cheek, wide and winding like the Mississippi River. His eyes were blue as the sky, and they glistened in the hazy light, and I saw it clear enough as a tear rolled down his cheek and wet his sideburns. Then another. And another. His mouth quivered. I never saw a grown man weep before.

"Oh Lord, what now? What now?" he cried, and I felt mighty embarrassed standing there, but what was I supposed to do? He had made an oath to the Confederacy to serve his time in the army with honor, and he'd broken that oath and run off. If he had anyone to blame for his troubles, it was his own fool self.

"I gotta place you under arrest," I told him, even though I knew he wasn't talking to me. Pa always said that a man who pities himself leaves no place for the mercy of others, so I figured I better just stop the man from his self-pity right away. It was for his own good.

"Oh Lord," he groaned and wept. "Oh forgive me, Lord."

"You committed a crime, and uh . . ." I felt real bad now, and part of me wanted to call Dash off the man, but he had tried to cut me with his knife. What could make a man so crazed that one minute he'd try to kill a boy and the next he'd be crying and begging the Lord for mercy?

"I'm gonna call the dog off, mister," I told him. "But don't you try anything, or he'll bite you again."

I pulled Dash off the man, and there was a big red spot where he'd ripped up the uniform and bit clear into the man's shoulder. Dash sat at my heel and looked up at me, tail wagging, panting with the excitement of it all. I patted his head.

He just wanted to know if he'd done good, and I guess he had. My first capture. I should've felt proud. Why'd I feel so rotten?

"Thought we'd lost you, Andrew." Winslow's round shadow blotted out the sun through the doorway and cast his dark shape across my prisoner. Winslow puffed and wheezed from running, and the eyes of the deserter on the floor went wide with fear. I didn't blame him much for that. Winslow's shadow against the sun looked like Cerberus, the three-headed dog from Greek myths who guards the gates of the underworld.

The sight gave me a start too. His shadow had two heads poking out from beside his proper head. I had to turn to see the two men standing on tiptoes to peer over Winslow's shoulders. The heads belonged to Rufus and his cousin Wade, and they jostled to get a view because this was their first deserter too, and they was anxious to see what he looked like. I could see their disappointment that he looked just like any other man, maybe a little more bedraggled and bloody, but he weren't no snake and he weren't no monster. Just a man.

Winslow looked him up and down and shook his head. "You're a sorry-looking rascal and an insult to the uniform of the great Army of Mississippi."

"Least I wore the uniform," the man on the ground snarled back. "Least I went to war. You Home Guard boys ain't nothing but draft dodgers and criminals, threatening folks and chasing down men who gave more in blood than you can ever imagine. I won't be judged by you, by none of you! Cowards, every one!"

In a blur, Winslow's hand came up with his Colt revolver and the gray steel flashed fire. Dash howled at the sudden blast, and my ears rang. A smoke smell tickled my nose. On the ground, the deserter from the Confederate Army still had his eyes open, wide with surprise, but his chest had been blown open, a shot right through the heart, and his blood sank into the earth floor, making the dirt black.

Rufus and Wade whooped and hollered, and I just stood with my mouth hanging open, staring at the dead man on the ground who'd been alive just a moment before.

"He woulda been hung as a deserter anyhow," said Winslow. "I just saved the judge some time." He turned and left the cabin, and I followed him out into the light.

"You're bleeding," he told me.

I nodded. I still couldn't find the words to speak.

"See?" Winslow said. "That man was dangerous. . . . Now let's get you home. You and Dash done good work for the cause today."

He stomped off through the woods.

Dash looked up at me, real confused. The dog was used to hunting, and when the gun went off, we usually came back with meat. He heard the gun, but we was empty-handed. Dash whined, and I had to scratch him behind his big floppy ears.

"It's okay, boy," I told him. "You done good. We got what we came for."

Winslow whistled while he led the way, but I didn't feel like whistling. Dash trotted beside me and I thought, no, hunting down a man ain't like hunting down a raccoon at all.

17

CHAPTER 3

PICKING BATTLES

Ma made a big fuss when I crossed the fence and trudged the long way up to our house. She took one look at my torn trousers and the bloody shreds of my shirt, and she about dragged me across the grass by the ear while Dash found his way under the porch for his afternoon nap. I swear, I could hear him snoring straightaway, even over Ma's shouting.

"I just knew it wasn't right for a boy your age to go off with those —"

"Don't say it, Jennie," Pa hushed her as he hobbled onto the porch on his crutch. "The Home Guard ain't to be trifled with."

"Andrew knows that what's said here at home is private," Ma told him, and she gave me a stern look, lest I disagree.

Pa snorted, and then he waved across the property to where Winslow, Rufus, and Wade stood. They knew they weren't welcome to cross the fence onto Pa's property. His hospitality didn't run in their direction.

We lived outside of town a ways. Pa had two acres boxed in with a fence, and there was a few good shade trees on the farm. Patches of grass grew here and there, some tall as my waist, and other places, the dirt was just as bare as Pa's head. There were rain barrels along the side of the house, and the windows were all glassed nicely, though there was a broken shutter I was supposed to fix, since Julius went off and Pa wasn't in no condition to take care of it. A few chickens pecked around here and there, always keeping their beady eyes alert on Dash, in case the dog got it in his head to give 'em a scare. Them chickens were lucky that most of the time, Dash got so tired, he couldn't be bothered to mess with 'em.

Ma held me at arm's length and clucked at me just like the chickens. She shook her head sadly. "It's just too dangerous, going after all that rabble," she said, leading me inside to bandage me up.

She served me some milk from our cow, Molly, and gave me a biscuit smeared thick with bacon grease, and she stared across the table at me with worry carved deep in her forehead. Her eyes were wet, and I knew she wasn't just worried about me, but also Julius and my Pa, on account of his bad back and his twisted leg. My poor Ma had no end of worries.

I decided it was best not to tell her exactly how I got hurt, or else she'd forbid me from going out with the Home Guard ever again, but while she looked me over, I felt a tug in my stomach, like all I wanted to do was tell her just exactly what had happened, about the chase and the no-good deserter and all the stuff he said about battle and fear and how he came at me with the knife and how they shot him dead right there where I could see it and how I didn't want to go back out hunting down men with the Home Guard.

I knew it was coward's thinking, so I shoved that biscuit in my mouth and chewed and chewed just to keep myself from talking. I'd said it myself: A hero don't shirk his duties just 'cause he's afraid. Me and Dash would keep doing our duty until the cause was won and those Yankees marched themselves back up north and let us good folks be. If Julius could do his part, then so could I.

Ma sighed. "At least you haven't lost your appetite."

"Boy's growing," Pa said. "I bet he grew a yard and half just last night and another this afternoon." He smiled wide at me, and though it weren't true, I liked it when he joked like that. I was growing, growing so fast my bones ached, and I was looking forward to the day I might just be taller than Julius, who stood a good head taller than Pa. If I grew fast enough, maybe Julius would have to wear my old clothes, instead of the other way around.

"You ready for your lessons?" Pa asked me.

My brain was buzzing like a hive of bees from all that happened that afternoon, but Pa insisted I read with him every day. He said a life of the mind was more important than anything. A man is never free of tyranny unless his mind is filled with wisdom, he liked to say. We were reading some old poem about a great war in ancient times, the Trojans in their city under siege by the Greeks. There were gods and generals and soldiers and their wives, all kinds of heroics in the story, and I liked it well enough, but he made me memorize whole passages and recite them back at him, and I would have much rather just read the book without being tested all the time on how much of it I could remember. Seemed to me like all his questions just drained the fun right out of the story, but he said we was training my mind, and that kind of thing wasn't *supposed* to be fun.

"Oh do give the boy a rest," Ma said. "He's had an ordeal today."

"Even more reason to study!" Pa objected, but Ma shook her head and clucked at him this time and, well, Pa never could argue with Ma's clucking. Like a good general, he knew how to pick his battles, and this was one he couldn't win.

He sighed and looked back at me. "Andrew, your Ma says you need a rest. That true, boy?"

I nodded, filling my mouth with the last bite of biscuit and licking the greasy crumbs from my fingers with loud smacking sounds. The biscuit and the glass of milk had restored my strength and calmed my thoughts. I didn't worry no more about that nasty deserter or the horrible things he said. He got what he deserved, and that was that. I knew Pa wouldn't see it that way, so I didn't tell him neither. They'd hear about my heroics soon enough, next time Ma went to market or Pa hobbled into town to get feed. I knew Winslow and Rufus and Wade would be at the saloons, drinking and bragging already, and maybe me and Dash would come up, our heroics talked about by grown men and old soldiers, like we were them ancient warriors Pa was so fond of. I smiled at the thought of it, and if my spirits were nudging upward, they started to soar at what Pa said next.

"I hope you're not too tired to read your brother's letter." He smirked an' held up a piece of paper with my name on it. It was folded over and sealed in wax.

Julius had written to me — my very own letter! Ma and Pa got one too, I was sure, but this letter was mine, and I almost jumped up and snatched it from Pa's hand.

"No, sir," I said. "I ain't too tired to read from Julius!"

My father chuckled. "I didn't think so." I took the letter with a thank-you and asked to be excused. I went to the little room where my bed was, and I shut the door and lay down. My back stung where I lay on it from the cut that deserter had given me, but the pain wasn't too fearsome bad, and I slid my finger under the wax and cracked the seal open, little red crumbles falling onto my stomach. I held the paper up to the window, and there was Julius's curling handwriting, all squiggly and cursive. He'd filled two whole pages, just for me.

Dear Brother Andrew, he began. *I have seen the elephant, as they say.*

Outside, I could hear Dash under the porch, burbling and whining as he chased down a raccoon in his dreams.

CHAPTER 4

THE LETTER

Dear Brother Andrew,

I have seen the elephant, as they say. We met up with the Yanks two days back, and this is the first chance I've had to set it down on paper. How I wish I could tell you these tales in person, lying under the shade of the willow tree, Dash snoring by my side, but the war goes on and neither North nor South seems ready to let up until all the killing's done. I begin to fear there is no way out but total annihilation for either side, for one side cannot win but the other shall lose totally. Many are losing heart. Just yesterday, I heard that twenty men from one regiment deserted, and we lose more every day. The roar of war deafens more than a man's ear. I fear the soul is lost somewhere in the din as well.

I have seen a man along the picket line before the battle so wracked with fear of the advancing blue uniforms across the misty field that he turned his musket on his self. He stood right beside me, and that one shot, aimed into his own brains, was the first shot of war I ever heard.

The sound was enough to call out others, and from his tragic blast, the fight began. Men screamed and charged, stepping over the man's body as we ran to meet the enemy. All around me, muskets blazed and cannons roared. The smoke was so thick on the field, only the orange flame of musket fire could be seen. The best I could do was stay low in my ditch and fire when I saw a blue uniform through the haze. I do not think I hit anything, man or beast. I do not wish to know. I saw one boy from our side, a boy no older than you, running in a brave charge ahead, when a chain fired from a Yankee cannon sliced him in half. The poor boy's legs kept running even as the top half of him flopped on the ground like a fish. I do not mean to sicken you, brother. Just to tell how I saw beside me in one hour's time enough death and terror for an entire lifetime. I am unhurt, in body, without in fact a scratch on me, save a minor powder burn from my own hot musket.

My thoughts, however, are awash in blood. I wonder why Pa's books of heroes never tell of the dreams these heroes have when they close their eyes at night to sleep, or of the sleepless nights that heroes must endure. Perhaps they do not suffer these afflictions. Perhaps it is only I who am no hero.

I do hope you are looking after Dash, keeping his nose on the hunt, and his spirits high while I'm away. I raised that dog from a whelp, and for some reason, of which its mysteries are beyond me, I find my thoughts go to missing him more often than I care to say. Ma and Pa and You and Home itself all seem in my memory tied up in a bundle with that hound dog, so that the thought of his bark or his fur or his cool snout nuzzling me is enough to send me soaring over the miles and settling back down at our house. I admit to weeping at the mere thought of it. Do not think less of me for this, Andrew. I find since these last several days, when my feet are sore and blistered and the smell of gunpowder still lingers in my nose, that I am brought to tears at the most inopportune times. I pass most of my waking hours alone now, away from the others in camp, so as to avoid the shame that salty tears can bring. While our cause is Just, I fear that hot lead and the cold steel of a bayonet care not. The hero and the coward meet the same violent ends. I can only hope to conduct myself with Honor if my time should come.

The last and most important question I have to ask you, brother, is this: Have you received word from the lovely, kind-hearted Mary Ward? I know, before I left, her family moved to the city, for fear their abolitionist ideas would place them in danger in our countryside. I know my heart should not call out to a girl with such Union sympathies, but love is like the wind . . . it blows wild where it will. My wind blows in whatever direction Mary's family has gone. Perhaps you are too young to understand. Has she sent word to ask about me? I must know. I feel I could bear all the horrors of the battles gone and battles yet to come, if only I knew that I remained in Mary's heart! Do you know what hope is like, brother? It is the flame that lights even the blackest night. Without it, there is only darkness. Please, brother, send word to me if you know these things I ask. I could cut through a thousand thousand Yanks to reach her window, if only with the hope to hear her sigh my name.

With affection and a heavy heart, your brother,

Julius

I set the letter down on the bed beside me, and I gazed out the window to think on what my brother had written. He wrote real fine, just like Pa taught us, and it was like I could see the things he'd written in my mind. I almost wished I had gone to study ancient war with Pa instead of reading these words from Julius on the present war for Southern independence.

I was all kinds of mixed up from the day. The deserter in the morning and the troublesome letter from Julius in the afternoon left me feeling all hollowed out and dried up, and I didn't know what to think. Julius wrote that they had twenty men desert from just one regiment, which made me mighty afraid they'd all come my way. Dash was sure up for it, but I didn't feel certain that I was.

I thought about writing Julius a letter in reply, but I didn't know what news to tell him. We hadn't heard from his girl, Mary, since her family packed up out of Meridian. They were sympathetic to the Union, and they were abolitionists too, which Pa said was no great fault of theirs. Slavery weren't no good, he said, but worse was the force the North used to enslave all the South. Pa could abide abolitionists, but Union men, like Mary's father, he could not abide. A lot of folks felt that way.

Julius had always kept his love of Mary secret, though I knew all about it. Until he left for war, we slept not a foot from each other our whole lives. He even carved her name in the side of the bed frame where he thought no one would notice.

When Mary left town, Julius got heartsick, and that was the week he joined the army. He figured, the sooner he could end the war, the sooner Mary could come back to him. But the war went on and on, and Mary hadn't sent any letters at all.

Dear Julius, I wrote him. *Dash is doing fine. We hunt almost every day. Food is scarce and Pa's back is acting up worse than ever, but we get by. Don't worry about us. When we ain't out hunting,* ~~me and Dash~~ *Dash and I help out catching deserters. We're real good at it, and just today we caught one and . . .*

I couldn't bring myself to finish the letter.

I went to sleep that night trying to think what things I could tell him to ease his mind, but it wasn't an easy time, and I had my own worryin' to do.

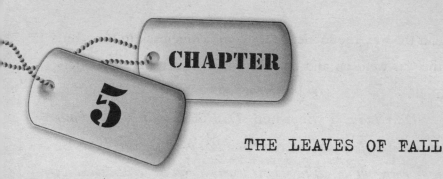

CHAPTER 5

THE LEAVES OF FALL

The air got cooler, the leaves changed colors, and the war went on. We got word from Julius from time to time, asking about this and that, talking about a skirmish here and a battle there, and every letter filled me with sadness to read about his own sadness. Ma and Pa wrote him back, but I couldn't find the words. He kept asking about Mary Ward, but she hadn't written to inquire about him, and I feared it'd break his heart to tell him so.

The Union soldiers were all around to the west of us, and everyone was mighty nervous for when they'd come to sack Meridian. Our home was right in their path, but Ma and Pa told me not to worry. From what they heard when Vicksburg fell to the Yanks, if you didn't own no slaves and if you treated the Yankee soldiers respectful, they'd let you be.

I didn't know how I'd treat them respectful if they came, especially on account of my work with the Home Guard, but so far, things was calm and quiet. Most days, I took Dash around with Winslow, checking up on folks and chasing down rumors. We hadn't found another deserter yet, but we heard tell of a lot of them.

Men kept coming as refugees to town, and we couldn't tell who was truthful and who had fled the army. I guess most deserters steered clear of Meridian because of what we done to the man that tried to knife me. I liked to think it was me and Dash keeping 'em scared away, but it was more than likely Winslow and his Colt revolver and the guerilla fighters that moved in and out of town.

Winslow spent most of his days with Wade and Rufus, going door to door to tax folks for the support of the Home Guard. Folks was hungry and he was too, and he got food from everybody here and there. I didn't feel so good about it. Pa always said that taxes were another kind of government devilry, and he had no use for 'em.

One day, out by Widow Parker's farm, Winslow took her last eggs to gobble up himself, and I told him I thought it weren't right to go taxing folks who couldn't afford it. Not when he had plenty to eat and they had not near enough.

"You don't like it," he said, "then you can go on home and let the men do their work. We'll call on you when we need Dash for workin'."

"What about me?" I asked.

"What about you?" Winslow grumbled as he chewed his tobacco and spat a fat wad in a brown puddle at my feet.

"You don't want my help? Just my dog's?"

Winslow chuckled, and I knew right off he didn't care for me at all. To him, I was just some boy. He wanted Dash's nose, was all.

"I'm fast and brave!" I objected.

"How's your back healing up?" Winslow asked, but I knew he weren't really asking, just making fun. My temper went up and my face turned red as a beet and that made Winslow laugh a big, guffawing laugh, and I couldn't put up with that.

I quit on him right then and there.

I whistled for Dash and we stormed off. We was through with the Home Guard and through with Winslow.

After I quit, I took Pa's old rifle out and spent my days hunting in the woods with Dash. We caught possum and squirrels storing up for winter, and one day I took home a mess of quail for Ma to roast. Thanks to me and Dash, we ate better than most, and whenever we had extra, Ma had me run it over to Widow Parker, who was about as thin as a railroad tie. She was mighty thankful, and she wished me well and asked after Julius. I told her he was doing good and giving old Billy Yank what for, and though it weren't exactly the truth, I figured it was close enough to tell it without feeling myself a liar.

It was one of those late autumn afternoons out hunting that Dash picked up the scent of blood. He let out a howl and led me over to a thorny bush, and I could see the little green spikes glistening red. Now it coulda been any kind of big animal that cut itself on that bush, and at first I thought that if we could track the injured beast down, maybe we'd eat wild boar that night, but then I saw bits of cotton cloth tangled up in the thorns and left behind.

I never heard of a wild boar that wore cotton clothes, except in a tall tale Ma once told me. My heart quickened in my chest, thumping louder than Dash's tail on the dirt of the forest. This weren't no tall tale. Dash's nose worked the edges of that thorn bush, and I knew all I had to do was tell him to go, and he'd be off after whoever left this blood and cotton behind. I feared it might be another deserter, and I didn't want to go after a man like that alone. The cut on my back had only just healed, and I was sure to have a scar for the rest of my life in a place I couldn't even scratch. I wasn't fixin' to have another.

But what if it weren't a deserter running hurt through the woods? What if it was another hunter, and he'd got injured and needed some help? I could track him down with Dash. Maybe I'd save his life. What kind of boy would I be if I didn't try to help an injured man on account of being afraid? Julius was chasin' down the whole Union Army, after all. I could go after one injured man. Dash and my Pa's rifle would protect me just fine. Least ways, that's what I told myself.

I patted Dash on his side, and he looked up at me, eager and slobber-lipped.

"Go git 'em, boy!" I shouted, and that was all the hound dog needed. With a high-pitched *"Aooo!"* Dash was off, paws beating the earth and nose working like a bellows on the blood-scented air. I chased right behind, and it felt good to run.

Dash ran so fast, I couldn't hardly keep up. It was his high-pitched barking and howling *"Aooo!"* that told me which way to go. When I finally got to him, he stood under a tall tree, barking up the trunk. The leaves had begun to turn red and gold, and they'd thinned out considerably from the height of summer so that the sun came through the branches and dappled the ground.

"*Aooo! Aooo!*" Dash said.

"I got it, boy," I told him, and I unslung my rifle. There was a bloody streak running up the trunk, and I followed it with my eyes to where the branches started, and I searched and searched, like I was looking for a raccoon hiding up the tree. Then I saw it, the curled-up shape of a person trying to keep out of sight in the crook of a big branch where the leaves was still thick. Every time he moved, a rain of yellow, red, and orange leaves spiraled down from the branch and settled on the ground. No foolin' those leaves. They gave his position away with their rustlin' and fallin'.

"I see you up there!" I said.

I heard no reply, but I saw the figure move, and it almost took my breath outta me. It weren't no deserter up in the tree, and it weren't no man either. It was a girl, her skin dark as a moonless night, her clothes all torn and tattered, her hair knotted and tangled with leaves and thorns and such, and her bare feet and legs bleeding something fierce.

I didn't need to have Pa's smarts to know what she was: contraband. That's what folks call a runaway slave.

She was the first one I ever saw, and it was my duty as a citizen of the South to bring her to justice.

CHAPTER 6

CONTRABAND

"**Y**ou gonna come down, or do I gotta shoot you down with my rifle?" I hollered up.

"*Aooo!*" Dash added, which made the girl curl even tighter into the crook of her branch.

"I see that you're bleeding," I told her. "You can't stay up there till Judgment Day."

"I ain't comin' down 'less you call off that dog," the girl shouted at me. Her voice was scratchy, but she spoke more clearly than I expected.

She didn't sound half as scared as the crazy old deserter who'd cut me a few months back. Runaway slaves weren't as bad as deserters from the army, I supposed, but they was still bad, stealing themselves away like that, when they was owned fair and square. I might even get a reward for bringing this girl back to her master. She'd probably get whipped something fierce in punishment, but she'd broke the law by running away. I'd be breaking the law if I didn't return her, reward or no. The law's the law.

Funny thing. We was fighting a war with the federals and they wanted to take away all the slaves in the South with their Emancipation Proclamation, and it occurred to me then that I hadn't never talked to a slave before, or any of their race, man or woman, young or old.

"How'd you hurt yourself?" I asked.

"Runnin'," she said. She didn't offer more explanation, and I guess I didn't care to ask. She stared down at me with her eyes shiny as black river stones, and I looked up at her for a while, but the sun coming through the leaves was like arrows shooting at me. Staring up made my head hurt. I slung my rifle back up on my shoulder, and I grabbed Dash by the scruff of his neck.

"Hush now, boy," I told him, and he did it, lowering his howls down to a whimper. "Sit," I told him, and he sat down on his hind legs, but I could feel his muscles all tight and ready to jump.

Dash didn't like unfamiliar folks. I pulled out the cord I carried in a loop and slipped it around Dash's neck to hold him back.

"There," I said. "I called him off. Now you come on down and surrender yourself."

"I'm coming down," the girl said. "But I ain't surrendering."

"You got to surrender," I told her. "I caught you."

"You ain't caught nothing!"

I blew a strand of hair out of my face and shook my head. This girl had me frustrated. I was wasting the whole afternoon on her. "I caught you!" I yelled, and my voice went and cracked again. I tried to cover it up by clearing my throat, but the girl let out at a laugh anyhow.

"You ran me up a tree," she said. "That ain't the same thing as catching me."

She had me there. I run enough raccoons up trees to know that they ain't caught until they caught. They were tricky creatures, raccoons.

I didn't know if girls was tricky like raccoons, but I couldn't well climb up after her, and I didn't want to take no chances.

"I got a dog and rifle," I told her. "So if I ain't caught you yet, it's just because I don't want to hurt you."

"You ain't caught me yet because I ain't let you catch me," she snapped right back. "Now, why don't you tie that dog up over there." She pointed to another tree trunk. "Set your rifle down beside him, and then I'll come down."

I looked where she pointed, then I looked back at her. Then I looked up and saw the sun had already started to make its way across the afternoon sky. It'd start getting chilly out here, and my stomach was already grumbling, and the sooner all this was well and done, the better. So I did like the girl said — not because I couldn't have caught her if I wanted, but because this way would be faster — and I tied Dash up and I set Pa's rifle down, and then I came back to the tree trunk.

She shimmied down in front of me and landed on the ground with a wince. Her left leg and her left foot were cut pretty bad.

"That hurt?" I pointed. She nodded that it did.

I wiped the sweat off my forehead and I thought on it. The girl was bleeding, and if I didn't get her fixed up before I returned her to her owner, folks might say it was my fault, that I damaged their property. I couldn't just let her bleed herself to death. If I saw a man's dog hurt by the road, I'd patch it up, and I figured the same was true for slaves. They was more valuable than dogs, certainly, even if they was harder to trust.

"Sorry, Ma," I muttered to myself as I ripped the sleeve off my shirt and came toward the girl with the cloth. Another bit of my clothes ruined.

The girl backed away.

"For the bleedin'," I told her. She took the cloth from me and tied it around the cut in her leg. She tied it real good, like someone had taught her.

"Who's your master?" I asked.

She didn't answer me.

"I said, who's your —?"

"I heard you!" she shouted, cutting me off. Then she stuck her chin up in the air. "But I got no master."

"Every slave got a master," I said.

"I am no slave." She grimaced as she pulled the cloth tight around her wound.

"You a runaway slave."

"My name is Susan," she said.

"And I'm Andrew." I sorta groaned it, because she was being difficult on purpose. "And that don't make no difference in the world."

She shook her head at me.

"Now you tell me, girl," I commanded her, the way I'd heard foremen command their slaves on the big plantations. "Whose property are you?"

"I said my name is Susan," she snapped. "And the man who bought me got killed in the war."

"Someone inherited his property, I'm sure."

"I'm nobody's property," she said coolly.

I didn't want to argue with her no more, but I had to figure out something. I couldn't spend all day in the woods talking with a runaway slave. We had to get going someplace.

"Well, where you come from?" I said. "Where'd you live before your master got killed?"

She didn't answer, just pressed her lips together.

I sighed. "I gotta untie Dash, I guess."

"Mobile," she said, because she didn't want me letting Dash loose. He was straining on the cord I'd tied him with and growling at the girl all the while. It was enough to make any stranger nervous.

"Mobile," I said. That explained a lot. She was from the city, probably serving in some fine house where she learned to talk smart and fix bandages and get civilized. I bet she even looked down on me for being a country boy. That made me mad, and I wanted to tell her off, but Pa said that rudeness was a sign of a weak and lazy mind, so I bit my tongue. "Well, I can't take you all the way back to Mobile. That's in a whole different state. How long you been traveling?"

She crossed her arms and didn't answer me. Best I could figure it, she'd run off and was trying to get up to Jackson, where the Union Army was. A lot of slaves ran off to find the Yankees because they took in the runaway slaves and wouldn't send them back. Guess the Yankees figured they could break up the rebellion if all the slaves ran off, but they had another think coming. My family did just fine without slaves, and all the emancipation proclamations in the world wouldn't break our fighting spirit.

"I gotta take you to the Home Guard," I said. "They'll know what to do with you."

Her eyes went wide when I said that. Her lip quivered a bit, and she glanced over my shoulder toward my rifle. She was scared, but she wasn't about to give up.

"Don't think about trying to get the jump on me," I told her.

"I'm stronger than you," she said.

"Dash'll protect me."

"Dash?"

"My dog."

"He's tied up."

"He'll break free if I'm in trouble, and if you run off, we'll just catch you again."

"You didn't catch me yet," she said. "I'm still free, ain't I?"

"Not for long." I took a step backward, closer to my rifle. I figured I'd need it. The girl was right: She sure looked stronger than me.

When I took a step backward, she took a step forward, keeping the distance between us the same.

"I ain't gonna let you get that rifle," she said.

I took another step back and she took another step forward, and then Dash growled. The girl stopped stepping toward me.

"Told you he'd protect me," I said. I took three quick steps back and picked up the rifle. The girl didn't move this time. She watched me, her face hard, like it'd been carved from rock. She looked like she was about to run, and I really hoped she wouldn't because I didn't want to chase her again, and I didn't want to hurt her at all, but she clenched her fists and I squeezed my hands around the rifle.

All of a sudden, the girl just crumpled where she stood, like a piece of paper in a fist. She curled in on herself and rested her elbows on her knees and her face in her hands and then she took to crying. I mean, weeping. She was just bawling there in front of me. Even Dash was startled. He sat back on his paws and cocked his head sideways.

"I — now, don't cry — I —" I didn't know what to say. I never knew much what to say to girls under normal circumstances when I saw 'em in town. I wasn't sure if I should yell at her or be sweet, like Julius said girls liked. All I knew was that I wanted her to stop her crying so I could place her under arrest. I lowered my rifle down and took a step toward her. I heard a rumblin' growl from Dash, but I ignored it. I squatted down in front of her. "Why're you cryin'?" I asked. "You sad for your master? Someone in Mobile'll take you back, I'm sure. A lot of folks need maids and such. And you speak real good. I'm sure you'll get bought up in no time."

"You don't know nothing about nothing, do you?" she spat at me, and I almost fell backwards.

"I —" I stuttered.

"I heard that folks was free up north, and the moment I reckoned my master was dead, I ran off to get some of that

44

freedom myself. My mother'd been sold off three years ago, and I'd given up hope of ever seeing her again. But then, when the war started, well, I got to hoping again. I thought maybe my momma would run to freedom herself. Maybe we'd find each other. My hope had nearly burned itself out, but a little spark lit up into a flame. I ran and I didn't stop for nothing. Days, I ran. And just when I thought I was close, I get caught up by some boy and his dog! You know what it's like to have your mother taken away from you? To lose hope? I come all this way only on the hope to see my mother again, and then, to see you? And to have my hope snuffed out?"

She wiped her tears away with her hand and looked away from me. Her words chilled me. I remembered what Julius said in his letter to me over the summer: *Do you know what hope is like, brother? It is the flame that no wind can extinguish. Without it, there is only darkness.*

How could a girl like this think the same big thoughts as my big brother? She weren't educated like he was, but she spoke real good. She weren't heroic, but she was brave enough to run from her dead master's house. The things she'd said wormed their way into my thoughts.

I could turn her over to Winslow, sure. They'd punish

her for running away, and then they'd probably take her back to her rightful owners or else sell her off again. They might even keep her for themselves. Or worse.

I pictured what Winslow did to the deserter, how he shot the man in cold blood. I thought about Julius, lying in his tent in some camp, or on the march through mud and the blood of Yankee armies, and I felt a churn of nerves in my stomach, like always when I knew I was about to do something wrong, and the knowing it was wrong wasn't gonna stop me doing it, anyway.

"Stay away from the train tracks," I said, backing away. Susan looked up at me, her head cocked sideways just like Dash's.

"What's that?"

"You gotta go thataway." I pointed. "But stay away from the train tracks because the Home Guard patrols them."

"You —" The girl stood. She wasn't so quick with her tongue now. I'd stumped her, and it felt good.

"Yeah, I'm letting you go," I said. "It's a sin, letting property steal itself away, but I'm a sinner, I guess."

Her face got all funny and soft-looking. Her eyes flicked over me, and a smile pulled the corner of her mouth. I don't know why, but I blushed with her looking at me like that, and I looked away and went back over to Dash, still tied up.

"You better go," I said, "before I change my mind and turn you in like I should."

She nodded and started to trot off. Then she stopped and turned back. "Thank you, Andrew," she said, real proper, like we was in some Mobile shipowner's tea parlor.

"If you get caught, you better not say my name again," I told her, and then she smiled for real, her teeth bright white in her dark face. I watched her run off, and I felt just about as low as I could. What kind of boy was I? Ripping up my shirt and then letting a runaway slave go? Helping slaves escape was against the law.

I untied Dash and we made the long walk home, with nothing to show for our hunt but a torn shirt and bellyful of guilt. I shook my head. I was just about the worst son of Mississippi there ever was.

THE HIGHER LAW

That night we ate a root vegetable stew with no meat in it, and even for that, I didn't have much of an appetite. I told Ma I'd snagged my shirt on a tree, and she sighed real big but took it off me to mend, and I got another of Julius's old ones to put on. It was a little moth-eaten, but it'd have to do for now, Ma said. I couldn't be trusted with nothing nicer. I kept my mouth shut, but I wanted to tell her I didn't deserve nothing nicer, not after how I'd let that girl escape.

After eating supper, I read my lessons with Pa, reciting some passage of that big old book about a hero named Sarpedon, a mortal son of the god, Zeus. When he died in battle, not even his powerful father could save him, so the minor gods of sleep and death came down over the battlefield and carried his body away. While I recited it, Pa had tears in his eyes, and it troubled my thoughts even worse than they was already troubled.

"What's wrong?" I asked him.

He shook his head and waved me away, and I figured lessons was over for the night, which suited me fine. I had my own troubles to think on. I went out to the porch and sat on the wood planks beside Dash, whose side rose and fell with heavy breaths. Every time he snored, his eyes twitched and his big ears flopped and his lips spluttered. Even his paws twitched. I was amazed the dog could sleep through his own sleeping, it was so loud.

I rubbed his side and I stared up at the stars in the sky. Julius was out there somewhere, fighting to protect our way of life, and here I was, safe at home, messing it all up.

I'd quit the Home Guard, and now I'd let a runaway slave go free. It was a bad crime, what I'd done. For all I knew, the girl would go spying on all our defenses and tell 'em right to that nasty Union General Sherman and his army of bums. She could be a spy or a witch or any wicked thing, and I let her slip away because I felt bad for her.

But everything I'd learned told me I shouldn't feel bad for her. I'd been told that the colored folks was better off under slavery, that the Southern civilization was good for 'em, and a sight better than how they lived on their own, all savage and brutish and whatnot. Some good Christian taught Susan to speak properly and to tie bandages, and for all I know, even how to read. What'd all the abolitionists do for her? Just made the war that killed her master and set her bleeding through the woods on hope.

False hope, if you asked me. Over the summer, we might've lost Vicksburg and Gettsyburg, but we was gonna win this war, and Susan and them folks like her was gonna be restored back to their rightful owners. Things were gonna go back to the way they was.

But even so. She cried for her momma.

I never did think the colored folks felt sentimental like we white folks did. I'd been told they didn't feel emotions like us, but she sure seemed to. She said words the same way Julius said 'em, and my brother was just about the smartest, most feeling boy I knew. If that runaway felt like he did, who could say she should be made to stay in Mobile if she didn't wanna? How'd I feel if I got my momma stolen away from me like that?

I'd feel like crying and running away, myself.

But that didn't change nothing. She was still a slave, and it weren't right for me to let her run off. It was against the law, and like the preacher said, it was also against the "natural order of things." So I'd broken man's law and heaven's law by letting her go. I was a criminal and a sinner.

But in the North, man's law had changed to wipe out slavery. And all those abolitionists, like Mary Ward's father, said they had heaven's law on *their* side, that all men should be free. North and South couldn't both be right, could they?

I felt sick about it. Any which way I looked at it, I done wrong. I done wrong against the law and against my brother's bravery and the Southern cause, and I done wrong against heaven, and I didn't even bring any meat home for supper. I sure wished Julius was around to tell me what was right.

Inside, I heard Ma and Pa whispering to each other, urgent and heavy with worry. Then I heard Pa's heavy footsteps on the floor, the *clomp, clomp* of his crutch as he came to the door and stepped outside. Dash woke up with a start and looked at Pa a long moment, then sank his head back onto the wood planks with a heavy thunk.

"Andrew," Pa said, his voice all grave and grim. My heart froze like winter ice. He knew what I'd done. I was sure of it. I was in trouble now. I swallowed hard.

"Yes, sir," I said, my voice cracking again. I could already feel the sting of the whipping I'd get for what I'd done.

"I have some terrible news," Pa said, holding a letter in his hand. "Your Ma thinks you ain't old enough to hear it plain, but I think different. I don't want no tears now, boy, understood? Your Ma has enough of those for all of us."

"Yes, sir," I repeated, this time at no more than the smallest whisper.

"Julius went missing after a battle with Union forces at Chickamauga," he said. "He ain't been seen since and his regiment fears the worst."

"No," I said. I didn't want to hear those words, didn't want to think 'em.

The worst: Julius, missing.

The worst: Julius, dead.

For some reason, I couldn't stop swallowing.

I felt Dash's wet nose on my hand. A dog knows when he's needed. His tongue licked my fingers. He knew something was wrong and thought to comfort me the only way a dog knows how.

But I didn't want comfort.

This was all my fault, I just knew it. I was no good. Pa didn't know nothing about my crimes, and he weren't gonna punish me for 'em. My punishment came from heaven itself.

I'd helped that girl steal herself away, so heaven saw fit to steal my brother away.

I know Pa told me not to, but I just started crying. I couldn't help myself. I bent down and pressed my face against Dash's neck, breathing in his dirty dog smell and just weeping into his fur. He didn't put up much of a fuss. He let me cry on him. I felt Pa's hand resting on my back, gently, full of kindness that I didn't deserve.

"I — I —" I started to tell him, to make a full confession, but he shushed me and he stooped down to my level, even though it pained him to do it.

"I haven't given up hope yet, Andrew, and nor should you," he told me. "Soldiers go missing all the time, and they turn up all the time too, sometimes with a different regiment, sometimes in a field hospital, sometimes — yes — as a prisoner of war. But missing is not the same as gone. Don't you forget it."

Then he pulled me away from Dash and held me to his chest.

"I'm sorry, Pa," I said, but he shushed me again and told me I had nothing to be sorry for. He just held on to me, and I knew his little speech was as much for himself as it was for me. I wanted it to be true, even if it wasn't. I wanted to hope.

CHAPTER 8

MY BROTHER'S KEEPER

I woke up next morning in my bed, though I didn't remember getting there. When I came out, Ma had cooked up some eggs and hoecakes and fried-up salt pork. I didn't think we'd had any pork in the house and figured she must have gone out to get it while I was asleep. I guess she needed something to do to keep her mind from running to Julius.

Even though I still didn't have much of an appetite, I ate the food. It was hot and it warmed me from the inside out.

Neither Ma nor Pa said anything, and the quiet was hard on me. I couldn't bear it, so I stood up, not knowing why at first. They looked at me, startled by my sudden move.

"I'm taking Dash into town," I said.

"How about you fix them shutters today?" Pa suggested.

"I got to go see Winslow," I told him. "Maybe he knows . . . something."

"Oh Andrew . . ." Ma put her hand over her mouth, distraught.

"I have to try looking," I said. "He's my brother."

"Andrew, be reasonable, now," said Pa.

"Or maybe I can help the Home Guard again," I told him. "With Julius gone missing, *somebody* in this family got to help the cause."

I glared at Pa and felt a swell of anger inside me. It was anger at myself, for what I'd done, but I'd turned it around and I threw it at him because he was at home while Julius was gone, and it should've been the other way around, if it weren't for Pa's bad back.

My words struck Pa like a blow. His face twitched, and I felt bad for it as soon as I said it, but words are like musket shots. Once you fire 'em, you can't take 'em back.

I didn't wait for Pa to holler at me, and I didn't stay to apologize. I knew if I started to apologize, I'd tell them everything, all about the deserter getting shot and the girl I let go and how Julius going missing was all my fault. So I stormed out to the porch and I whistled for Dash.

It took most of the morning to walk into town. When I got there, the streets were bustling with men in the gray uniforms of the Confederate Army, preparing the defense of the city. They wore beards and many of them smelled something awful, but their officers looked mighty fine overseeing them, with pistols and swords, tipping their hats when ladies walked past.

A few slaves were at work building fortifications and digging trenches, and they hummed some colored songs to keep time with their shovels. Dash walked by my side and eyed the slaves warily. I heard him let out a low rumbling growl and I made him hush. The men eyed him as he passed, but they didn't stop their humming or break the rhythm of their digging. The soldier with the whip standing over them had his eye firmly fixed on their labors. I guess he feared they'd run off, just like Susan had.

Working under the hot sun like that'd make me think of running off too.

I avoided the soldier's gaze. I knew he didn't know about Susan, but I still felt ashamed to meet his eyes. The city needed every worker it could get, and Susan had looked mighty strong, strong enough to swing a shovel. Did slave girls do digging work like the men? Had I robbed the city of a worker it needed? Had my crime made our defenses weaker?

I shook my head. Surely, one runaway slave girl weren't enough to make the Confederate States lose the war. No, my crime was much smaller and the punishment for it was personal. Not the fall of my city, just the loss of my brother.

"Come on," I said, urging Dash along.

With the soldiers in town, there wasn't much for Winslow and his friends on the Home Guard to do. The army officers frowned on them taking food and supplies from ordinary citizens and didn't like them running about causing a ruckus. I knew where to go looking for Winslow in his idle times. I didn't like to set foot there, but I didn't have much choice.

The saloon.

At least I had Dash with me to scare off the drunks.

Standing by the entrance down a side alley, I could smell the stale smells that drinking men carry with them. There was moonshine and sweat and tobacco and all kinds of other, even worse smells. Dash stood rigid next to me, his nose working on all those sour scents, one paw lifted off the ground, with a sharpness in his eyes, like he was out in the woods on a hunt. He knew where we was headed was filled with danger. I stepped inside and the good dog stayed right with me, even though he didn't normally follow me into buildings. Like I said, a dog knows when he's needed.

It was dark and the air was hazy with smoke. Men spoke in low, grumbling voices. Three men with hats pulled over their faces played cards at a table in the corner. An old man stared into an empty cup beside the window, dreaming some private dream. As soon as I took two steps inside, the barman yelled at me: "You take that dog and get! This ain't a place for dogs or boys!"

All the grizzly faces turned to me, and I felt like I'd made a big mistake coming here. Dash felt the threat of the place and did what came natural to him. He started barking.

"I said get!" the barman yelled. Dash didn't take kindly to his tone one bit. Barking, he lunged for the bar, and it took all my might to catch him and hold him back. I slipped the cord around his neck and pulled him quickly outside, but I didn't scold him. I liked that he'd seen fit to protect me. I liked it a lot. Dash had been the only one to witness me let the slave girl go, and he still cared for me. That was something, anyway. Ain't no crime too great that a dog can't forgive you for it. Sometimes I think dogs are a whole lot better than people, at least in that regard. I wished I could forgive myself as easily as Dash forgave me.

"What are you doing down here, Andrew?" Winslow had peeled himself out of the saloon and stood blinking in the sunlight in front of me. His cheeks were red and he looked unsteady on his feet. I didn't see Rufus and Wade, but I was sure they were inside too.

"I came looking for you," I said.

"We ain't seen you in a bit," Winslow said. "Figured your Pa kept you away on account of us *patriots* not being suitable companions." He stumbled for no reason and caught himself on the wall. Then he glared down at me, almost daring me to mention his near-fall.

I didn't dare.

"What can I do for you, sonny?" He smiled real big, his crooked yellow teeth stained with tobacco juice. "Ready to take Dash out and hunt us a runaway slave?"

I almost gasped, but I contained myself. He didn't know about Susan. He couldn't know. He was just making talk.

"My brother's gone missing," I said. "Fighting in Chickamauga."

"And?" He spat. "What do you want me to do about it? Your brother's the *hero* after all." He spat the word *hero* like it was a curse word. Then he laughed a cruel laugh, and I regretted coming down this way at all.

"I thought you might . . . know something?"

His whole body rumbled with laughter and his red cheeks tore open with a gruesome grin. "Oh Andrew, oh! That's a good one! Me? Know somethin'? You and your brother are the ones with book learnin'! I don't know nothin' at all!"

"I meant about my brother," I said. This conversation was even more frustrating than arguing with the slave girl. At least she talked sense.

"I don't know nothin' about that." He shook his head. "These *regular* army boys don't think much of old Winslow, I'm afraid. My service don't count for much in their eyes."

Now he'd made *regular* sound like a curse word.

"You best go to talk to them. I was you, I'd start at the hospital on the hill," he said. Then he held his finger up for me to wait and disappeared back inside. He came out after a minute, stumbling, and he held a tin cup out to me. "You might want this before you go. Fortifications."

I leaned forward and sniffed the cup. Whatever liquid he had in there smelled like it could melt the ties off a railroad track. I held my hands up and thanked him. Said I wasn't thirsty just then, and me and Dash backed outta that alley just as fast as we could.

Winslow stood there with his cup out, watching us go and muttering curses all the while. I guess my Pa was right all along. The farther I kept away from Winslow, the better off I'd be.

But he had been helpful in one way. Now I knew where I needed to go, though I dreaded it worse than the saloon.

I had to go ask about my brother at the army hospital.

As we climbed the hill toward the big brick building that had once been the finest hotel in town, I saw tired-looking nurses step outside to take in fresh air. One of them was dabbing herself with some kind of perfume in a little glass bottle, and I quickly came to understand why.

I felt bad for Dash. Even to my human nose, from fifty feet away, a mob of stinking smells assaulted us, and the closer we got, the stronger the smell of human misery rose up to repel us. Though my thoughts screamed at me to turn back, my legs pushed forward to the door.

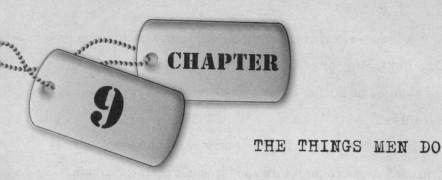

THE THINGS MEN DO

"**E**xcuse me, ma'am." I approached the nurse who'd doused herself in perfume as polite as I could. She eyed my raggedy shirt and my hound dog and raised an eyebrow at me.

"This is no place for dogs," she said.

"I'm looking for my brother," I told her. "He fought at Chickamauga."

"Why, son, that is over three hundred miles away!" She shook her head at me. "We're treating the wounded from just ten miles around. General Sherman's on the rampage, and you think your brother'd come through all that to our little hospital? How do you expect he'd do that?"

I shrugged, not really knowing distances, myself. Hearing her say all them miles of fighting between where Julius gone missing and where I stood, I felt my own hopes draining away. I almost wanted to collapse right there, but I bit the inside of my cheek and puffed up my chest and forced myself to keep on hoping. Julius got lost, so he wouldn't be any place a person would expect him to be. Otherwise, they couldn't say he was lost. I figured then, he must be someplace a person wouldn't expect him to be. And a hospital three hundred miles away from the battle he'd fought seemed as unexpected a place as any.

So I told myself, anyway.

I wondered if the lies you tell yourself count as lies.

"Well, you can't bring that dog inside," the woman said.

"Sorry, Dash." I scratched his ear and tied him to a hitching post.

"Not there," the woman scolded me. "That's where they bring the wounded in! Tie him up by that tree."

Dash grunted when I pulled him over to the tree. He'd walked a long way into town and wanted to lie down. "I'll be right back," I said. I don't reckon he could understand me, being a dog and all, but just the same, it felt good to talk to him. Calmed my nerves for going inside.

Dash flopped himself onto the ground in the shade of that tree and took to sleeping straight away. I was mighty tired myself, but I marched back over to the front door, past the nurse who smelled of lavender perfume, and stepped inside.

The smells that assaulted me were nothing compared with the noises. Men coughing and groaning and talking and praying. There were screams of agony where surgeons worked as well as the wheezing breaths of consumptives fighting for air. Nurses and doctors spoke in hushed tones, but the patients themselves didn't bother with quiet. There was too many of them, anyway.

Those who could stand stood all around the room, leaning on canes and crutches, leaning on one another, bedraggled and bandaged, with bruises colored like the leaves on the ground outside. Others sat against the walls of the long hall, side by side. I saw men with oozing bandages on their heads, men missing hands, and men missing feet. Rows of beds and stretchers lined the center of the room, and they were crowded too with wretched figures. I saw one soldier on a crutch standing over a bed and telling a nurse the name of the man lying there, just before he pulled a sheet up over the soldier's head. Not a moment later, the body was hauled from the room by two slaves, and another soldier took its place, clutching his arm where the flesh hung off like ribbons. They didn't even change the bedding for him.

The nurse who smelled of lavender was suddenly beside me. She shook her head sadly. "The things men do to each other. I swear, it's enough to break your heart."

"It's for a good cause, ma'am," I told her.

"You believe that?"

"I do," I said. "These men are fightin' for freedom and our way of life."

She sighed. "I'm not sure any cause is worth the suffering we've seen in this war, on both sides."

"They started it!" I objected.

"You're young," the woman said. "In time, I pray boys like you will understand what a war does to the bodies and the souls of men, regardless of who started it."

"I understand just fine," I said, because I didn't care to be lectured at by this nurse.

She looked at me real sadly and wished me luck finding my brother.

"You best check on that list there." She pointed at a wall covered with papers. Each paper was covered with names. "That's the register. If he's here, he'll be on the list." Then she walked away to tend to the wounded some more. Everyone else was either too busy dyin' or too busy attending to those that were to pay any mind to me.

I walked over to the list and ran my finger along it. The writing wasn't real neat, but I could make out the names. *Michael Amberson, Charles Anderson, Daniel Anderson, Jonathan Anderson*, and on and on, name after name, sorted in alphabetical order. I scanned the *B*s, where Julius should be, but his name wasn't there. It was a relief to see he weren't in the hospital, but sad too. I was hopeful I'd see him and I could run home and tell Ma and Pa that he was okay. But I figured the battle where he'd gone missing was a while back now, and maybe they didn't keep records up on the wall that long. Maybe there was an office someplace with the old papers. As much as I didn't want to stay in that hospital a moment longer, I came all this way to find my brother, and I couldn't give up so easy.

As I walked to the far end of the great hall — it used to be the ballroom when the place was a hotel — a man on the ground reached out and grabbed my leg.

"You see the elephant yet, boy?" the man snarled up at me. He was a cavalryman, or at least he had been, to judge by his uniform and riding boots, but his face was badly burned, and one of his eyes was sealed shut with the scarring. The other eye, dark and piercing, moved around wildly.

"I . . . I . . ." I stammered. "Not yet," was all I could think to say.

"We need men, you know. Take the fight to 'em. Yanks will have to kill every man, woman, and child before we let 'em take the South!"

"Quiet down, John!" another patient shouted from down the hall. "Some of us are trying to sleep until the war's over."

"You best get out there, boy," the man whispered to me. "War's a young man's game, and you're a young man, no? Get out there and fight the good fight! For honor! For dignity!" He was shouting again. "For the Great State of Alabama!"

"You're in Mississippi, sir," I told him as gentle as I could.

"I am?" His burned face wrinkled.

"You are," I said.

"Well, what do I care about Mississippi?" He coughed and spat on the floor. "Leave me be, boy." And with that, he shoved me away.

I went on down the great room and turned into a smaller room.

I sure wish I hadn't.

I saw a table laid out, and on it, a man, and he was screaming, with an injured leg all cut up and yellow and oozing something awful. The room smelled like rotten meat left out in the sun too long, sour and sweet at the same time.

A surgeon stood beside the table while two other soldiers held the man down. One of them gave him a slug of whiskey and a musket ball to bite down on. That's when the surgeon raised the blade of a saw and took it to the man's injured leg like he was sawing a plank of wood. I turned away and slammed my eyes closed. The man's shrieks were like no sound I'd ever heard before, even in my worst nightmares, and though I wasn't lookin', my mind painted pictures of the horror that could produce such a sound. I felt hot and dizzy, and I needed to get outside. I needed to get some air.

"Ow, watch out!" the man from Alabama yelled as I ran past. I'd stepped on his foot by accident, and looking back to mumble an apology, I tripped over another man, and he grimaced and his terrible teeth flashed at me, all bloodstained and broken. I caught myself on the wall and accidentally pulled down a sheet of paper from the register with all the names on it.

Mulligan, I saw as it fell, and *Masterson* and *Nathanson*. All them dead men. The papers rustled as I trod on them. I ran, leaping over men like Dash leaps over logs in the forest, and I raced for the door and the air and the light just as fast as my two legs would carry me.

CHAPTER 10

TOTAL WAR

I didn't rightly know where I was when I heard birds chirping and smelled the heavy scent of lavender. I blinked into the sun and saw the giant, droopy face of my dog, Dash, hanging over me. His flat, pink tongue licked straight up my face and over my forehead so my hair stood up with his drool like wheat standing in a field.

"Get up, boy!" he said, with a lady's voice. "You got to run on home now! Run home!"

My eyes must've bugged out of my head, because I ain't never heard a dog talk before, and if I were to think on it, I'd never figure Dash to talk in a sweet lady's voice. I'd gone crazy.

"Huh?" I pushed myself up off the grass onto my elbows, and Dash turned his head away. That's when I saw the lady standing behind him, the nurse who'd made me tie him up before. She was the one doing the talking, which I took as quite a relief. I sat up on the ground, brushing the grass from my shoulders. I felt like a fool for swooning, and for thinking my dog had been talking to me. Next thing the nurse told me, though, made me forget all about feeling foolish.

"General Sherman's here, son, and his men are burning everything!" the woman said. "They're headed this way! You have got to run on home!"

That made me hop to my feet, and what I saw was a frightful sight. Nurses were loading up all the men who could be moved onto carts and wagons. The men were piled on top of each other, groaning and weeping. Those who could walk on their own feet were walking in a steady stream out of the hospital. Some were fleeing in full retreat, leaving the hospital defenseless. Others pushed their way onto the waiting carts. I saw the burned man from Alabama hobble out and knock other, sicker men aside in his hurry for a ride to safety. So much for fighting the good fight. So much for honor and dignity.

In the other direction, down the hill and into town, what I saw was like a nightmare. It was afternoon, but the sky was black as midnight with smoke and ash.

Plumes of black smoke and fingers of orange flames rose

from all the factories in town. The saloon was burning, as were the storehouses and the homes of all the folks that lived on the main street. Citizens ran to and fro, trying to douse the flames with water, but the blue-uniformed Yanks in the streets stopped them and tossed their buckets to the dirt. Off toward the west, I saw the train station on fire and the tracks all twisted and tied. More Yankees held the line on the edge of town, cutting off any chance of a counterattack from the Confederates. I looked about, but couldn't see a single gray uniform anywhere. All the Confederate soldiers had gone and left us on our own.

I saw a river of slaves marching toward the Yankee lines on the edge of town, a hundred, two hundred, three hundred, and more, all of them walking away, heading to join the Union. I guess they all figured to steal themselves away while they had the chance. One man's loss is another man's gain, I suppose.

Yankee officers on horseback watched the chaos from the other side. And I saw one of 'em point our way, directing a group of soldiers up the hill to the hospital, with their torches blazing.

"Why?" I cried.

"It's total war," the nurse explained. "The Union doesn't just want to beat the armies of the South. They want to beat the fight out of every Confederate citizen. They aim to break us, and I fear they just might." She shook her head. "You take care and get on home."

She went to help more patients flee the hospital.

I looked beyond the edge of town, in the direction of home, and there too I saw the plumes of smoke rising, gray ghosts carrying the living up to meet the dead.

"Home!" I said aloud, and I untied Dash and we was running fast down the hill. We stayed off to the side of town so we didn't run into any of those Yankee soldiers on their rampage.

No one paid me and Dash much mind as we ran, but I saw them clear as day, and what I saw filled me with anger hotter than all the flames that burned my town. I saw officers and regular enlisted men in blue looting and stealing from the homes they burned, women crying as their dresses was tossed in the streets; stores of food stocked up for winter trampled underfoot or stolen away. I saw men not in uniform robbing and stealing like they was doing the Yanks' job for 'em, and I even saw old Winslow carrying off some silks from the general store. I put it all out of my mind, though, and just ran faster than I'd ever run before.

It still weren't fast enough.

Just down the road from our property, I saw three Union men in their dark-blue uniforms running away, hollerin' an' whoopin'. One of 'em, a mean-lookin' fella with a thick brown beard and a big scar on his forehead, was carrying a small box under his arm. I recognized it right off as the box where Ma kept the silver candlesticks that her Ma had given her, and her Ma's Ma before that.

I made a move toward 'em, but they all had pistols and swayed like Winslow under the drink, so I knew it'd be deadly to me and to Dash to face them down. I had to pick my battles, and I knew this was one I couldn't win. The men didn't take no notice of me, like all the other adults I'd seen, and they went right on by.

When I got to our house, there weren't nothing left but a smoking heap of ash and timber. All our things were gone, burned or tossed across the yard in heaps. Even the fence was trampled flat. Ma stood weeping with her hands over her face, and Pa limped from heap to heap, poking through the piles with his crutch to separate what could be useful and what was ruined altogether.

"Oh Andrew," Ma cried out when she heard Dash barking our approach. She ran to me and embraced me, crying.

"What happened?" I shouted. "What'd they do this for?"

73

"They say we was all guilty of harboring the rebels," Pa sighed. "A whole troop of federals came by and gave us just a minute to pack our things and step outside before they went in and took what suited them and burned the rest. They even took old Molly." He sighed. "General's orders, they said. Apologies, they said, but her milk belongs to the Union. Everything we own belongs to the Union, they said. They were polite about it, which made it all the worse."

In that moment, Pa looked to me like an old man for the first time in my life. He looked like he'd been left out in the sun too long, and had wrinkled up and dried.

"What'll we do?" Ma wept. "Where will we go?"

Dash sniffed around in the ash piles, pawing at the timbers that was left of our house. I wondered what he was looking for. A familiar smell? A piece of the porch to lie down under?

"Ain't nothing left to find!" I yelled at him, 'cause I had to point my anger someways. "Ain't nothing left at all!"

Pa just shook his head. "We can go stay with your cousin Thomas," he said. "He'll put us up."

"We never asked for charity in our lives," Ma said.

"What choice have we got?" said Pa, and I knew it hurt him to say it. He bent down with considerable strain and picked up a burned piece of paper from the ground, a page from his beloved old poem about the war between the Trojans and the Greeks. It weren't even readable no more. At the sight of that, even Pa broke down weeping.

I felt about as low right then as I had ever felt in all my life. It was all my fault, I just knew it. This was my punishment for letting that girl go and for not telling no one about what Winslow'd done to that deserter and for just being a lousy, no-good coward like I was. Julius had gone missing and Pa was crying and our whole house in ruins, and I should have been here, instead of being passed out under a tree because the sight of blood had scared me so.

"How will Julius find us if he comes back?" Ma asked, worry written across her face like it'd been carved there since ancient times.

"I guess we can leave word with the neighbors — those that stay, anyway," said Pa, but it sounded like even he thought it wasn't much of an idea.

Dash came back and sat at my feet, whimpering up at me, hungry and thirsty, just like I was.

"I don't got nothing for you, you dumb dog," I scolded, and that's when I had me an idea. Dash weren't my dog to begin with. He belonged to Julius! And if Dash could track a stranger through the forest, well, he could certainly track down his rightful master!

I looked up at Ma and Pa, gathering what they could for the journey to Cousin Thomas, and I puffed out my chest and spoke loud and clear. Without my voice cracking once, I made my proclamation. "I'll go find Julius."

"What's that?" Pa looked up. Ma's mouth hung open like fresh caught fish.

"Me and Dash are the only ones who can do it," I said. "I'll go find his old regiment and ask around, and maybe Dash can pick up the scent. We've tracked down all kinds of folks before, we can track down our own kin."

"You can't go off doing that," Ma said, but Pa didn't say nothing for a while. He just looked at me for a long, long time.

"Boy's right," Pa said at last.

"No, Paul." Ma turned to him. "He's just a child."

"War makes boys into men before their time," Pa told her. "Always has been that way. If Julius lives, we need him more than ever. I'm too old to go over the countryside searching for news, and Andrew's a smart boy. He'll do all right. Besides, it don't do no good to have him sitting around with us in despair. Don't do no good at all."

I nodded, eager. I felt like, finally, it was my turn to be a hero. I could track down Julius and bring my folks good news in a world that'd turned full of bad.

"I just know he's alive," I said. "I know it."

Pa sighed. "So it is with men: One generation grows on, and another is passing away." Those were lines from his big *Iliad* poem. Though the pages had burned, his memory still held on to them. "Let's see what we can scrounge up for the journey," he added.

Ma set her jaw to keep from crying, and she went looking through the wreck of our house for provisions.

"You be careful, son." Pa told me. "You stay away from the boys in blue, and if you hear shootin', you run the other way, understand me?"

I nodded.

"You know where Cousin Thomas lives?"

I nodded again.

"Well, you make your way there in two weeks' time, hear me?" Pa said. "No matter what."

"I will," I promised, and I scratched Dash behind the ears. His tail wagged because I guess he knew that we was going off on the biggest adventure of our lives, and if we found success, maybe we could just set things right again and make up for all the bad we'd done.

CHAPTER 11

THE PREACHER

Ma loaded me up with a satchel filled with all the food we had left, even though I told her I'd be fine to scrounge as I went.

Pa was sorry he didn't have his rifle no more, but the Yankees took that from him too, in case he were gonna use it to help the Confederacy.

"I'll find Julius, and we'll give them Yanks what for," I told him, but he just shook his head sadly.

"Two weeks," he reminded me. "You come on down to Cousin Thomas's in two weeks."

They watched me walk off down the road, Dash trotting at my side. I took the long way around town, but it didn't matter much. It looked like all the Yankee soldiers and all the bummers and runaways who followed them had hightailed it back the way they came. I felt a lot of anger that they'd marched right through town without encountering a fight from our boys. Our soldiers had retreated at the first sight of blue uniforms, and they was only just now starting to trickle back.

"You know where the Fifth Mississippi Infantry is?" I asked one line of men as they made their way past me, but they just shrugged. They didn't know nothing, and I feared I'd be wandering the countryside aimless for the whole two weeks before I had to turn around. There was no way I'd find my brother's regiment just by asking folks down here. Even if they knew, they'd most likely think I was a spy.

I had to be near enough to Julius for Dash to catch his scent, which meant I had to do some figurin' about where he might be.

I walked and thought all the way into evening and hardly noticed when I'd come to a road all filled with folks. Some carried bundles and some hauled trunks. Some were wounded and some looked sick, but they was all fleeing the destruction the Yankees had left in their path. There must have been two hundred people gathered along that lonesome country road as the sun set on the longest day of my life so far.

By the time it was dark, the roadside and the fields beyond were dotted with campsites flickering with little fires. Folks roasted bits of meat or ate corn cakes and sipped at weak tea. They chewed tobacco and spat and coughed. A few in the crowd wore the uniform of this or that unit of the Confederate army. My eyes bulged, and Dash growled. There was deserters on the road, just about as open and free as could be.

The sight of it made me mad, and I thought about setting Dash on 'em, but I figured we was all tired from the day we had, and I didn't know their stories. Maybe they weren't deserters at all. Maybe they were heading to find their own units to get back in the fight. If Julius was out there, lost, I'd want him to have a campsite to lie down in safely for the night.

I declared a truce then and there in my head that I wouldn't hunt no deserters until I found my brother safe and sound. I'd already let a slave girl go, after all. If these men was deserters, it didn't make no difference. I couldn't bring them to justice *and* escape justice myself, not for the crime I'd committed.

I approached a small fire beside a wagon hitched to a sorry-looking mule. There was just an old man and a black boy a little younger than myself sitting cross-legged by the fire, roasting up a measly few squirrels they'd caught. The old man wore the collar of a preacher, and I took comfort in that, so I asked if I might join them for a spell.

"You on your own out here, son?" the preacher asked me, and I said no, sir, I had Dash with me, and he took to laughing at that in a real kindly way. "Why don't you stay more than a spell?" he suggested. "We got room around our fire for one more, and the roads at night ain't no place for a boy an' his dog on their own. Bandits at large, son. A lot of dangerous folks come out in dangerous times."

"Thank you, sir," I said, sitting down by the fire, just as darkness settled over everything, heavy and smoking from the burning day.

"Call me William," the preacher said. "And this here is my boy, Alfus. He don't speak, but he listens nicely, and I'm sure he's tired of my voice going. I'll bet he's glad to have another voice to hear just about now."

The dark-skinned boy smiled and nodded, watching the fire with a sparkle in his eyes. I'd never sat round a fire with a dark-skinned boy before, but I'd never lost my home or walked the road alone with Dash before neither, so I figured it was a day for firsts.

"I'm Andrew," I said to the preacher. "And this is Dash."

"Pleased to meet you." Preacher William stretched his limbs. "Where you headed?"

"Well, sir," I said. I had to think on it. "I guess I don't know. I'm looking for the Fifth Mississippi. My brother fought with them, you see, and I'm trying to find him, on account of our house being burned. He's gone missing, they say, and I think my dog and me — I mean, my dog and I — can track him."

"The Fifth Mississippi?" The man rubbed his chin. "I travel all over these lands, spreading the gospel. Let's see. . . . I do believe they're fighting under the army of Tennessee right now. The command post is just a day or two's ride to the east of us. Their officers will surely know where to find your brother's regiment."

"Really?" My face cracked a wide smile. It was the first good news I'd heard in ages. I hopped to my feet.

"Slow down, young Andrew." The preacher raised a hand in the air. "You need your rest. Why don't you camp here with us for the night, and in the morning, I'll ride you over myself."

"You sure?" I asked, taking my seat again. "I don't want to be any trouble."

"No trouble at all," he said. "The Lord's work takes me wherever I'm needed, and I imagine their officers have need of a preacher as much as anyone else at times like these."

I was glad to hear it, and I imagine, if he could understand a word of it, Dash would've been glad too. Dogs don't like to go on long walks for miles and miles, especially not hound dogs like Dash. He was tuckered out already and snoring in a floppy heap of fur at my side. The ground was hard, but Dash's fur made as soft a pillow as I could ask for. I slept about as well that night under the stars as I'd ever slept in my life. I was sure that soon, I'd find my brother, Julius.

CHAPTER 12

POWERFUL FRIENDS

I rode with the preacher all the next day and into the day after. Dash sat beside me in the wagon, watching the people on foot. We passed more burned farms and scorched fields, and to see the land I loved turned so desolate just about broke my heart. It was like every place a field was burned, a little piece of hope had burned up with it.

Preacher William fed me and told me stories about his travels, how he preached to the troops at Vicksburg and at Jackson, how he moved from regiment to regiment, all over the land, spreading hope and prayer to all those who needed it, and how folks was sufferin' but their hearts was strong.

"You see a lot of battles, then?" I asked him.

"Oh yes," he said. "I have seen the elephant."

"Were you scared?"

"My faith gave me courage," he said, "as it gives all men in times of trial."

"We sure are having a time of trial," I said.

He nodded gravely. "We are indeed."

I asked him, "You think we'll win this war?"

He considered it a long, long time while the mule dragged us along. It looked like Alfus was listening carefully for the answer too. "I don't know if anyone rightly wins a war," he said. "And this war, well . . . I don't think either side knows what winning is anymore. When elephants fight, it's the grass that suffers."

"The grass?" I asked. I didn't really understand him. "Like all the burned fields?"

"And the people who tend them," he said. "We're the grass. Our towns, our people."

"You don't believe the war is just?"

"I'm a pacifist, Andrew," he said.

I didn't know what that was, but I didn't want to embarrass myself by asking. I guess he could tell, though, because he just went right on and explained it.

"A pacifist is a person whose conscience will not allow him to bear arms or to kill. My faith tells me that all lives are sacred. The lives of white men and of slaves both." He glanced down at Alfus. "The lives of Southerner and Northerner, man, woman, and child. I bear no ill will toward my fellow man and will not bear arms against him for any cause."

His words sounded like treason to my ears, but he was such a nice man, and I didn't want to insult him, so I kept my mouth closed and thought on it. He sounded an awful lot like the nurse back in the hospital. In fact, it seemed to me, the folks I'd met who'd seen the most of war were the least inclined for it.

But our cause was just! I knew that to be true, and some things had to be worth fighting for, no matter if they was dangerous or bloody. Pa's big book about heroes said so, and Julius said so, and everything I'd ever learned said so. I guess, for the preacher, things was different, but I weren't no preacher and didn't intend to be. I was ready to fight for my home and to send those Yankee invaders running scared back to where they'd come from.

I didn't say anything else because I didn't want to get into an argument, and anyway, we started to see more and more soldiers on the road, and pretty soon we was the only ones on the road who weren't soldiers. I looked at the big men with thick beards and tattered gray uniforms with wonder.

These were the heroes! These were the ones fighting the good fight!

They all looked mighty tired. They didn't cast friendly glances up our way.

Suddenly, an officer in a wide-brimmed hat, his chest all pinned with medals, approached on horseback and ordered us to halt. He had a waxed mustache about as wide as the brim of his hat, and his shining sword dangled at his side all the way down to his polished boots in silver stirrups. He looked like a fine gentleman, and I was pretty excited to meet him.

"What's your business?" he snapped, and there was nothing fine or friendly in his voice.

"We've come to minister to the Regiment," Preacher William said, removing letters from his cloak and passing them down to a foot soldier, who ran them up to the officer. The officer studied the pages with a raised eyebrow. He looked us up and down.

"You know President Davis?" the officer asked.

The preacher nodded, and my eyes near bugged out of my head. He carried a letter from Jefferson Davis, the president of the Confederate States.

The officer grunted. "We ain't runnin' a Sunday revival here," he said. "You can go on, but keep your preaching confined to those who want it, and when the orders to march come in — and they will come in, I tell you — you best get out of the way double-time or we'll run you over, no matter whose letters you carry."

"Understood," Preacher William said, and goaded his mule. The officer handed the letters back as we rode by, and Preacher William tucked them into his cloak. He gave me a wink. "A man of conscience may still have powerful friends . . . or, at least, letters that present such appearances."

"You mean —?" I startled. "Them letters was fake!"

Preacher William smirked. "In the business of saving souls, a little stagecraft is often required. My harmless fraud might just help you find your brother, after all."

"Hmpf," I grunted, and crossed my arms. The preacher was a sneaky one. I figured I'd better be rid of him soon, before I got painted with the same brush. I was here to find my brother, not play tricks on the army with a pacifist and his boy.

Just as soon as we reached the Regiment, I saw the big white officers' tents set up and rows upon rows of filthy lean-tos where the enlisted men made camp. I hopped down from the wagon while it was still rolling. Dash gave a bark and jumped down behind me.

"Thanks, Preacher William!" I called back. "Good luck saving souls and pacificizing and all that!" I waved as Dash and I ran off toward the big tents of the regimental headquarters, and if William called after me, what he said got lost on the breeze, 'cause I didn't hear it.

CHAPTER 13

A CLERK'S WAR

I tried to seek out someone to help me, but the soldiers ran to and fro, just about as busy as a hive of bees, and I couldn't get no one to pay me any mind. I saw officers strutting, shouting orders, and men in all manner of dress grumbling about those orders. Not everyone had on the proud gray uniform. Some wore yellow coats and others had on tattered blue ones that they must've taken off Yankee soldiers. Some men wore broad straw hats to block the sun, and others had on no shoes and went about dirty-footed with raggedy trousers dragging in the mud. This was not the look of any army I expected, but times was rough and soldiers made do.

I worried that Julius was out there somewhere, lost or hurt, without shoes on his feet. I hoped, wherever he'd gone, that he had the good sense to keep his shoes.

As I walked the camp, Dash sniffed around the area. He went right on over to a big artillery mounted on wheels, where men stood about smoking pipes and studying maps in the glaring sun, and he lifted up his leg and marked the wheel of that big gun like it belonged rightly to him.

"No, Dash, no!" I scolded, and ran over to him, but the men who saw him do it burst out laughing.

"Who's that dog think he is?" one of them said over the laughter. "General Johnston?"

"No one below the rank of colonel can pee on this here gun," another called out.

"I guess we better salute him!" said a third, and they all carried on cackling.

I apologized and slipped the cord around Dash's neck and pulled him away from the big gun. He followed along, panting happily, like he didn't have a care in the world.

I crossed a big open space where the ground was all torn up by footprints. It must have been an area for running drills, but no one was using it now and I marched Dash around it a few times to make sure he didn't have to take care of no more of his bodily necessities. I found a corner tucked away behind one of the big officers' tents where I could take care of my own too.

As Dash and I stepped back into the open, I saw a tent across the way with its flaps wide open to the breeze and a gauzy light coming through the canvas all around. In the center of the tent was a wooden desk, where a clerk in a gray uniform worked busily on stacks of papers.

A dark-skinned fellow in a pressed cotton shirt and fine striped trousers came into the tent with even more papers and set them down on another table and left again without a word. After him, a young lieutenant came in and set more papers down.

"Casualty reports, sir," he said, and the clerk nodded and the lieutenant bustled out again. I watched for a while as soldier and slave alike came in and out, giving over papers to the clerk. Some of them announced what they was bringing, supply lists or receipts of goods or official letters from the generals or more reports of casualties from battle, and the clerk would direct the men where to set the papers down, but even as he did, his scribblin' never ceased, and he barely looked up to acknowledge the men or the papers they brought for him.

I never thought it before, but not all the business of war was done by soldiers fighting in the field. Some of it was done by clerks at desks in gauzy light, squinting over blotted ink and shuffling papers to and fro. I ain't never heard of a grand, old poem about the heroism of clerks, though, but I guess wars can't get fought without 'em.

I figured that if anyone would have some knowledge about what happened to my brother Julius, it'd be the clerk with all the papers, so I strolled right over and stepped inside the tent, with Dash's cord held tight to keep him from getting into trouble. He sat down at my feet like a soldier at attention, and I was real proud of how that dog carried himself. Taking his example, I stood up extra straight too, feeling a bit like a young soldier myself.

"Excuse me, sir," I said, loud enough for the clerk to hear. He looked up fast and sized me up, then bent his head back over his papers. I felt like I was always in this position, stepping into rooms, trying to get adults to notice me. Even standing up real straight and proud, I couldn't get their attention. I was just about to shout for the clerk, when Dash took care of it for me.

"*Aooo!*" he bellowed, and cracked the quiet air of the tent like an ax through rotten wood. That brought the clerk's head up real fast.

"I'm trying to find somebody," I said to answer the expression of surprise and confusion that the clerk threw at me and at Dash, who'd taken to wagging his tail in a most unsoldierly way. "Can you help me, please?"

"I don't have time for this." The clerk waved me away and went back to his papers. I thought about setting Dash on him and making the man help me, but that was just 'cause I was tired of having to convince adults to pay notice.

"It's my brother, sir," I said, trying to keep my patience. "He's gone missing . . . and Pa's sick . . ." I didn't want to lie to the clerk, not for something so important. Pa really wasn't all that sick. But I wondered how much I could stretch out the truth so this man would help me. Was it okay to lie if it was for a good reason? I guess that's why the preacher used them fake papers. He and I weren't so different after all. But I thought I'd put a little more truth into things instead. "The Yankees came and burned our house, see —"

"You from Meridian?" the man asked, and he had real sympathy in his voice now.

"Just outside it, sir," I told him.

"I heard about General Sherman's raid," the man said. "Terrible. He'll pay for his cruelty one day, I'll tell you that. We'll avenge your loss and that of every good Southern family!"

"Thank you, sir," I said, glad he'd warmed up to me. At last, someone who believed in the cause without all that hemming and hawing. "I'd really like to know, if you keep records for this kind of thing, about my brother. We'd heard he'd gone missing and, well, I come looking for him with our dog, here. I guess, before I got to searching, I wanted to be sure he wasn't . . ."

"Dead?" the clerk said.

I nodded.

The clerk tapped his fingers on the desk. "Name?" he asked.

"I'm Andrew," I said.

"Not your name," he clucked. "Your brother's name. Full name, if you would be so kind."

"My brother's name is Julius Burford," I said. "From Lauderdale County. He was with the Fifth Mississippi Infantry, I think."

"Tarnation, son, what makes you think he'd be all the way down here? They fought up in Tennessee!"

"I know that, sir," I said. "It's just that, like I said, he's gone missing and I thought . . . maybe he turned up closer to home?"

The clerk stood, grumbling, and crossed the room to a table piled high with more papers. He rummaged through them until he found some kind of list and held it up to the light that streamed in through the canvas of the tent.

I stood, waiting, my heart thumping in my chest. I didn't know what sort of list he was studying, but I feared it might be a list of the dead. I shifted my weight from foot to foot and listened to the sounds of the military camp outside — songs and curses, laughter and oaths of all kinds, and a heap of thunderous snoring and whinnying of horses. It seemed to me a military camp was a mighty loud place to be. All the sounds had Dash turning his head this way and that, his big jowls flapping with every snap of his neck.

"I see," the clerk muttered to himself, and then looked up at me, nodding, a thoughtful expression on his face.

"Is my brother on that list, sir?" I asked. My voice cracked again.

"He is," the man said gravely.

"Is that . . . causalities, sir?" I imagined telling Ma the news, telling Pa. What words could I use to tell 'em that all hope was lost? Julius would never come home again.

"This?" The clerk looked at the list like he was surprised to be holding it. "No, son, this is not casualties." He sat down again and leaned back in his chair. The wood creaked beneath him. I felt a wave of relief come over me. Julius was on a list and he weren't dead. "Andrew, was it?"

"Yes, sir," I said.

"Andrew, I don't know how to say this nicely, so I'll say it plain." He set the list down on top of his other papers and pointed at it. "This here's a list I get every month of men to be on the lookout for, in case they turn up."

"So it just says that Julius is still missing?" I was disappointed, but at least I could still hope my brother was alive.

"No," the clerk said. "This is a list of men who left their post and shirked their sworn duty before their term of service was over."

"You mean —?"

"Your brother is a deserter," the clerk said, and if he said more than that, I didn't hear him, because the blood was buzzing in my ears, and I saw the pictures in my mind of the deserter I'd run down with Dash, the coward who'd knifed me, the coward that Winslow'd shot dead in the cabin by the railroad tracks, and when I saw him in my thoughts, he wasn't the red-bearded fellow I remembered. He had Julius's face.

For a moment, I wished the clerk had told me that Julius had died in battle, a hero's death. Instead, the clerk had told me that my brother was a no-good coward, the kind of man who deserved to be chased down by dogs.

"No," I said, and I felt my blood running hot. The air in the room felt heavy, and I struggled to breathe. "No," I said again, and I stumbled from the tent.

I was outside again, Dash at my side. If Julius really had turned deserter, then the Home Guard would probably be looking for him somewhere. If somebody like Winslow found him, well, Julius would be in a world of trouble. I shuddered to think it.

But if I found him first . . .

I was the only one who could do it. I *had* to do it. I could make sure no one hurt him. I could bring him back to his regiment, and I could make him do his duty to defend our freedoms! I could find him and make him the hero he was supposed to be, and that way, I'd never have to tell Ma and Pa how he'd been a coward, run off just like all them cowards who ran off while our home and our town was burning.

I knew why I'd come all this way. I knew how I could make up for the crime of letting that girl Susan get away. I wasn't meant to find my brother to bring him home.

I was meant to find my brother to bring him back to the war.

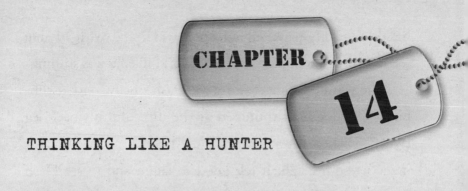

CHAPTER 14

THINKING LIKE A HUNTER

I didn't know where I might begin to hunt for my brother, but I thought that maybe someone in the big military camp might've known him, so I took Dash around to the rows and rows of small lean-tos where the enlisted men were laying about, cleaning their guns, playing cards, and boasting of this or that. Again, no one paid me much notice, but they did take a shine to Dash straight away.

"Woo-ee," said one young private, who had the accent of a Texan. "That there's a mighty fine hound. Mighty fine!"

"Best hound in all of Mississippi," I told him, and I let him rub Dash's head, which Dash liked quite a lot. In fact, he liked it so much, he took to flopping right down on the ground and rolling over on his back for a rub on his belly. Dash's big lips flopped upside down and his ears splayed out on the dirt beside him, his paws spread open wide, and with his big teeth showing, it looked to all the world like he was smiling.

The private laughed and gave Dash's belly a good rubbing. The dog's tail thumped at the dirt, and his back leg twitched when the private hit his ticklish spot, and that made us both laugh. It felt good to laugh and to see Dash happily rolling in the dirt. Took my mind off my worries for Ma and Pa on their way to Cousin Thomas, and off Julius, on the run from the law and from his rightful duty.

The thought of Julius made me lose my smile real fast. "You know if the Fifth Mississippi Infantry is in this camp?" I asked the private. "Or any folks who fought at Chickamauga last September?"

"Chickamauga?" The private stopped rubbing Dash's belly and met my eyes with a steely stare. "Well, son, I don't know about the Fifth Mississippi, but I sure fought at Chickamauga under General Gist. Our brigade lost 170 men in under an hour, and I tell you, it was a most fearsome sight. Men falling all over each other in the fight, and then falling all over each other worse in retreat. I ain't ashamed to say I was scared in that battle, and if I don't see another like it, that'll be just fine with me."

"My brother was in that battle," I said. I left out the part about him turning deserter. "I'm trying to find folks who might know what's become of him."

"Gone missing, eh?" the private asked.

I nodded.

"A lot of that going around," he said, and I wasn't sure if he meant a lot of men deserting their service in the army like my brother did, or if he just meant it like he said it. He didn't explain and he didn't pry, and I took that as a kindness.

"Me and Dash are gonna find him," I said, and that made the private smirk a little.

"Listen here," he told me. "Best thing you can do, if you want to find someone who maybe, for whatever reason, don't want to be found, you gotta think like him. You ever use this hound of yours to hunt raccoons?"

"Well, yes, sir, I have!" I said real proud, because Dash was the best coonhound in the state.

"Well, when you hunting raccoons, you start just by letting him run off after whatever his nose can find?"

"No," I said. "I start by going to the right spot, like a creek bed or a corn patch where the raccoons sometimes forage, and then I let him loose."

"Exactly," the private said. "So think of your brother like a raccoon right now. He's runnin' scared —"

"I didn't say —"

The man held up a finger to hush me. "He's runnin' scared, like a raccoon. Where do they go when you're chasing 'em?"

"Up a tree," I said. "Or they burrow into the ground."

"That's right," said the private. "So where would your brother's burrow be? Where he run up when he runnin'? Back home?"

I shook my head. He hadn't run back home after all this time, and now, even if he did, there weren't nothing there to run back to.

"So where else might he find himself a little piece of safety?"

My eyes went wide, because right then, I knew it.

Miss Mary Ward.

My brother had such a fancy for her, like he had said in his letters, and if he was gonna hide, then that's where he'd go. If I wanted to pick up his scent, then that's where I'd have to start. The only trouble was, Mary Ward's family had gone to Jackson, which was in Union hands, and between me and them was the Union Army that'd gone and burned my house.

"I see you've got an idea," the private smiled at me. "That's good."

"But I don't know how to do it," I said. "It's a long way away, and Dash can't walk that far and I can't either."

"Where abouts you need to go?"

"Well, I —" I didn't think I should tell the man from Texas that I needed to look for my brother with Union sympathizers in Jackson. It was bad enough he'd figured out Julius had turned deserter. It'd be worse if he knew that I thought my brother had run to the Yankee side. That'd make him look more like a traitor than a coward. But I didn't have no good answer to give him. I just stood there dumbly with my mouth hanging open, trying to think of something to tell that weren't a complete lie. I guess Providence figured out a way to spare me the lyin', because just as I was stuck on what to say, a trumpet took to sounding and that sent Dash howling, and suddenly the whole camp was all aflutter with activity.

"Hurry, boys, hurry now!" a sergeant shouted, running through the rows of tents. "Marching out! We're taking it to the Yanks now! Marching orders! Form your ranks!"

The private started fumbling with his jacket straightaway. He grabbed his musket and stood tall above me.

"They're playing my music," he said. "Looks like it's time to dance."

"Sir?" I said, because I wasn't sure why he'd be talking about dancing all of a sudden.

"We're on the move," he said. "And you best get out of camp before you're dragged into battle with us. They're always looking for drummer boys your age."

I knew some boys from town who'd gone off with the army as drummers. They march in the front of the columns of soldiers and beat their drums to keep time. Because they're out front, it's often them that get hit when the first shooting starts. Of all the drummer boys I'd known who went off to fight, ain't one come back yet.

"Cannon fodder," Pa used to call 'em, like they was food for the cannons. I didn't want to be cannon fodder, so I thanked the private and rushed to get out of that camp just as fast as I could.

Men shuffled from their tents, loading gunpowder in their satchels, muttering prayers and oaths, and lining up as their officers took to shouting. The whinny of horses and the clatter of metal made for an even more clamborsome noise than before. I listened for drums, but didn't hear none and that made me move double-time toward the gate, because I didn't want someone gettin' ideas on enlisting me, not when I had to go after Julius.

"Hey, boy!" someone shouted, and my blood froze in my veins. I stopped and Dash stopped right beside me, and we turned to see an officer of the cavalry, sitting tall astride a massive gray mare with a flowing mane of brown hair. The horse stood stock-still and the officer on her back just about glowed in the afternoon light. His mustache was dark black, like his eyes and the polish of his boots. He wore a broad hat and his brass buttons shone. I felt a swell of pride that a man like that should even notice me, and I hoped, for just one blink, that he *would* ask me to join him in battle, to carry the drums and lead the charge of the cavalry.

"That's a lovely dog," he said. And then he didn't ask me to join him. Instead, he said, "How much you want for him?"

"Sir?" I asked.

"The hound," he said. "I should like to take a fine dog like that into battle at my side."

Of course he didn't have no interest in a scrawny kid like me — he wanted Dash to fight with him. It were just like Winslow and the Home Guard again, and I got mad. My face must've turned to red, because the officer raised his hands in the air and laughed.

"Now, don't fret, son, I was only asking," he said.

"Thought maybe you could use some money for your family, and I could use a fine hound dog. I meant no offense."

"Dash ain't for sale," I said.

"Well, you take care of that dog, son," the officer said again. "A good dog is a soldier's best friend."

"I'm not a soldier," I said.

He just winked at me, then he turned his horse away. "Not yet!" he called back as he rode to review his troops assembling for the march into battle. I turned the other way and moved off.

"Andrew!" I looked to the gate and saw Preacher William and his boy, Alfus, riding their wagon from the camp again. "Come along, now! Riding beats walking!"

I trotted to catch up as I heard a bugle blow and then, finally, the sound of drums. They had a drummer boy after all, and I was strangely disappointed now that they hadn't called on me to do it, even if I had never banged a drum in all my life.

Dash jumped onto the preacher's wagon with one leap, and I climbed on after.

"Where you headed, Andrew?" the preacher asked, and I thought of lying again, but then I figured, I had no other ideas on how to get where I needed to go to chase down

Julius, so I might as well ask. A sneaky pacifist could be just the man to get me through the Union lines. Worst the preacher could do was say no and toss me from his wagon for having a cowardly traitor for a brother. I guess that weren't the *worst* he could do, but I didn't figure a man of God would do me more harm than that, especially not since I had Dash for protection.

"Well, sir," I told him as we put the soldiers and the camp behind us. "My brother's in a spot of trouble, and I aim to set him right . . . only, to do so, I gotta go over to Jackson."

"Jackson, eh?" Preacher William studied me. "I believe the Union Army is in control of Jackson now?"

I nodded grimly.

"Well, I suppose you could say we're headed that way ourselves," he said at last, and urged his mule on.

"Doing the Lord's work up that way?" I asked.

"You could call it that. Yes, you could call it that indeed." He smirked, and I can tell you I didn't like the look of it one bit, but I rode on because I needed help, and this pacifist preacher was the only help I had. Well, him and Dash. A hunting dog's time is the hunt, though, and we weren't at that time just yet. But we would be, and soon.

CHAPTER 15

CROSSING THE LINES

The country changed as we rode west. Rolling fields gave way to hills and then back to farmland again. We bumped along roads that'd been torn up by a thousand or more boots from soldiers on the march, and we passed by farms where not a soul was living, so burned and broken they were. I saw fences toppled by battle and the earth scarred from fighting, but in our ride, day after day, I didn't see a soldier anyplace.

When we was tired, we slept, and when we was hungry, we ate. Preacher William talked on and on about this and that, but to tell the truth, I didn't have a mind to listen. Some men just like to hear their own voices, and I figured the preacher were one like that.

It was the end of the third day since I'd left home, and I knew if I was to keep my promise to Pa, I'd have to turn around in just a few more days, so I was worrying over that when we made camp for the evening and I didn't notice the dark figures coming from the shadowy woods. Dash noticed 'em right quick though. He took to barking and howling, which sent three shadows scurrying away again, but a fourth stood tall and still, his back straight and an ax in his hand.

"Call off the dog," he said, and I could tell by his voice he weren't a white man. I called Dash to me, not because the fella told me to, but because I didn't want Dash to get hurt by the business end of that ax. The three other figures peeked out from the darkness and Dash growled, but I held him tight at my side. I knew he wanted nothing more than to charge 'em. I couldn't blame him none. I'd have wagered a dollar a Sunday for the rest of my days that these four was all runaway slaves headed to join up with the Union Army.

"You got nothing to fear from us, friend," Preacher William said. He stood, his hands open. "We are traveling servants of the Lord, and you are welcome to share our fire if you wish."

"They's runaways!" I whispered to Preacher William, but Alfus gave me such a glare that I hushed up fast.

That's when I realized that he too was a runaway, and that Preacher William weren't just a regular man of conscience, but an abolitionist, helping slaves steal themselves away. He was as good as a robber, sneaking the property and wealth of the Confederate States away in the night, and he'd gone and made me a conspirator with him.

I thought on Susan, the girl I'd let go myself, and now, here I was, traveling in the company of another runaway, and about to camp with four more of them. I felt like a traitor, just as bad a traitor as Julius, in fact. I wasn't making up for his cowardice at all. I was only making things worse!

"All men are created equal," Preacher William scolded me, and his face looked real stern when he said it. "I take those words to mean what they say and I do not abide the enslavement of any man. If you think different, Andrew, I urge you to reconsider or to find yourself some other conveyance to Jackson."

I didn't like to be scolded like that, not in front of all these dark-skinned folks. I'd memorized the Declaration of Independence because Pa said I had to in order to be a good citizen, so I knew where that line of the preacher's came from. The whole first part went "We hold these truths to be self-evident, that all men are created equal, that they are endowed by their Creator with certain unalienable Rights, that among these are Life, Liberty, and the pursuit of Happiness."

Like I said, my Pa didn't approve of keeping slaves our-selves, but I never heard him say them words from the Declaration applied to slaves too, and I guess I never thought of it before. I'd only ever known things the way they was, with the dark-skinned folks serving the white-skinned folks. Slavery was always the way in Mississippi, and all the preach-ers I'd ever heard said that was the way it was always meant to be. But now, this pacifist preacher was telling me it weren't meant to be that way at all.

I thought on the girl I'd let go, and how I felt bad for her out there looking for her mother, and it made me wonder if maybe I'd become an abolitionist myself. The thought was almost too terrible to think on. Ever since I'd seen Winslow shoot that deserter that me and Dash caught, I hadn't been right in the head. I'd been lying and I'd been shirking my duties to the Home Guard, and now, worst of all, I was thinking on helping even more slaves run off on their mas-ters. I wondered if maybe once you start to turn bad, you can't keep from turning bad all the way.

I sat down and looked away to pat Dash and rub his belly while the runaways joined our camp. Dash wasn't com-fortable, and I can't say I was either. I guess the runaways was about as uncomfortable as me an' Dash. They kept their distance and didn't say nothing but "thank you" when the preacher gave them food.

For his part, Preacher William didn't say nothing else, neither, and I think he was disappointed in me. Seemed like no matter what I did, someone was disappointed in me. The only one that I could count on was Dash. I kept him close as I drifted off to sleep.

We were roused in the morning by the sound of horses coming up the road, and the runaway slaves, all but Alfus, jumped up and hid. Dash barked after 'em.

"Quiet your dog up!" Preacher William yelled at me, his voice mean like I hadn't heard it before, and I thought it weren't right for a man of God to go yelling at me like that, but I held Dash on his cord so he didn't run off after the men. It was against nature to hold a hound dog back from the chase when every muscle in his body is crying out to run, but what could I do? I was at the preacher's mercy if I wanted to find Julius. The only way I could set things right would be to bring Julius back to the war. Every wrong I did along the way would be made right if I succeeded. I felt that the fate of all the South rested on my success.

The horses rounded a bend in the road, and when I saw the men with them, it sent a shiver up my spine. They were all Union soldiers, dressed in blue. There were two horses leading a column of men on foot, and the marching men numbered in the hundreds, with still more officers on horses riding among them and again at the rear.

"Hello there!" the preacher called out to them, raising his hand in a friendly greeting and stepping straight out into the middle of the road. The officers stopped their horses, and orders went down the line for the whole column of men to stop. A river of blue came to a halt before the preacher's raised hand, and I felt a moment of admiration for the man.

I saw the runaways peeking out from the woods as the preacher reached into his jacket and removed a letter. I inched closer with Dash tight at my heel to hear what was being said. It made my blood sizzle to be so close to Yankee soldiers. For all I knew, they was the same ones that burned my house to the ground and sent the whole town packing, but I wanted to know what trick Preacher William was up to now, so I moved in.

The officer on the horse in front studied the letter that Preacher William had handed him, and then he looked the man up and down. "This so?" he asked.

"It is," said William. "We've just come from the rebel camp not three days back and they were on the move, heading west with a full force. Upward of a thousand men, and a regiment of cavalry as well."

At that I almost screamed, but I bit my tongue. Preacher William was a spy.

He'd gone into the Confederate camp under a lie and spied on all the movements and now he was telling these Union officers what the Confederate Army was up to. I thought of the private from Texas and his fear of another battle. Thanks to this so-called pacifist preacher, he'd walk right into one!

The officer nodded. "We'll send a rider to let the general know what you've seen. Good work."

The preacher smiled, pleased with himself and his treachery, and then he pointed to me and I froze. Dash sensed my fear, and his body went rigid as a statue too.

"I wonder if you could offer us a kindness in return," the preacher said. "This boy here needs to find his way to Jackson. . . . I do wonder if we might find safe passage in that direction?"

The officer burst out laughing and Preacher William looked confused. I did too. I didn't know what the man found so funny and I didn't like the tone of his laughter.

"Jackson's just a half a day's ride down this road," the officer chuckled. "And I daresay you'll find safe passage.

That's about all you'll find. We've burned most everything else and sent the rebels packing, along with anyone who'd aid them."

The preacher paled. Even though he was a traitor, I guess he didn't take to men laughing at violence they'd done, like war was a joke. I suppose on that score, the preacher and I agreed. Maybe I was more like him than I'd thought. I'd let a contraband get away. I was sneaking over enemy lines. What made me better than him?

We stood still and watched the Union soldiers march past us, and I shuddered to see 'em up close.

They looked just like the Confederate soldiers, except for their uniforms. They wore the same style mustaches and beards. Some of them wore no hair on their faces at all. They looked about as old as Julius, and some looked even younger, about as old as me. A few nodded politely, others ignored us altogether, lost somewhere in their own thoughts. If it weren't for the color of the uniforms, I couldn't have told you the difference between a Confederate solider and Union soldier.

I can't say that was a comfort to me. They was just regular boys, and even so, they had burned up towns and left decent folks to live in ruins. I wanted them to look like monsters, and they didn't.

CHAPTER 16

DOG FIGHT

After the column of Yanks passed us by, I rode on with the preacher and the runaway slaves into Jackson. The four runaways sat in the back with me and Dash. Dash kept his eyes fixed on 'em, and they kept theirs on Dash. I couldn't get my dog to look away. He just couldn't relax around runaways.

I didn't say a thing to any of 'em either. Too many words had confused my thinking. I didn't want to think no more. I just wanted to find Mary Ward's house and fetch my brother and take him back to where he belonged.

Everyone, I figured, should just go back where they belonged, and maybe then all this mess would get better. The bigger the world got and the more people I met in it, well, the more confused I got about things I thought I knew for sure.

"War makes boys into men before their time," Pa had said. I hadn't even seen the war yet, not really, and I already felt about a hundred years old.

The road was scorched along the sides, and all the fields was burned. All the houses too. Along the road, I saw three dead bodies, lying facedown in a ditch, with bloody holes in their jackets where they'd been shot. I didn't dare look closer when we rolled by because I could hear the flies buzzing on 'em, and that's a sight no one should ever see.

If anyone else was left behind, they must've hid themselves at the sound of the mule clomping along, because we didn't see another soul until we reached Jackson.

The city wasn't in such bad shape. On the outskirts we saw the fortifications and the trenches all wrecked from when the Union overran the place. Soldiers in blue now held the works where once the brave boys in gray had stood guard over the city. They must have heard we was coming because the preacher didn't even have to stop the cart to show his letters. We just rode right in.

A few buildings had been ruined, burned down to charred timbers, but most still stood, and folks scurried about on the streets. Not in big numbers, but enough that I didn't feel afraid we'd wandered into a graveyard.

As we rode in, people turned to look up at me, the boy with the dog and all the runaways. I felt like they were judging me, thinking I was some kind of Yankee myself, so I told the preacher to let me off, and I'd find the rest of the way myself. He stopped the wagon and I climbed down with Dash.

"I wish you success, Andrew," Preacher William said. "I see a good soul in you, even if you don't yet know it's there. When the time comes, I know you'll do right."

"I'm doin' right," I said, and I whistled for Dash as we walked away again from the preacher and his contraband cargo. I realized I'd have to ask someone where the Wards lived, but all the people looked pretty distrustful of me. The folks I saw looked away as I approached, and even if I called out for 'em, they didn't respond. Having soldiers coming and going and ransacking your city makes a person close up to strangers, I guess.

I had to walk a ways to where the houses got farther apart. The sun was sinking lower to the horizon and I didn't want to get caught out in the streets when it grew dark. I saw signs posted about a curfew, which said that any folks on the street after dark would be shot as Confederate spies. I guess I *was* kind of a Confederate spy now, since I intended to take my brother back to fight for our side. Maybe, I figured, my spying would cancel out the preacher's spying, and things would balance out, like on a scale. Or maybe all my plans would just make things worse.

Dash and I trudged down a dirt lane where the houses were set back a ways and each one had big white columns and shady porches, and even the smallest one was grander than any house I'd ever seen in Meridian. If Mary Ward and her folks was still around, this would be the place for 'em. They was rich as King Midas. As I walked, I saw that most of the houses were dark. A few had broken windows, and one I saw had its front door torn right off its hinges. The lane was quiet as a tomb. All the rich folks must have fled when the Yankees came to town.

I took to feeling mighty hopeless then, and things only got worse. Dash stopped in the middle of the lane, and I had to turn around to call him forward. He wouldn't budge. He'd lowered his head and pointed his tail and the hair on his back bristled up. He let out a rumbling growl, and I wheeled about to see where he was lookin'.

Four dogs, mangy mutts that looked more wolf than hound, came stalking from the other direction. Their hair was bristling, and they was growling too. A big black one in the front of the pack had only one good eye. Where the other eye should be, there was just a closed-up spot where he'd lost it, either to sickness or violence. I didn't care to know which.

I stood between Dash and the pack of strays. I couldn't move my feet to run.

But old Dash weren't about to let a mangy pack of mutts make him afraid. My brave dog let out one earthshaking bark and, like the ancient hero Achilles rushing into battle, he charged at the pack, streaking past me and straight at the big black dog, knocking the brute into the dirt. The other dogs leaped on him in a flash, and the pack kicked up a storm of dust and fur. The sound of snarls and barks could've curdled a demon's blood, it were so fearsome. Through the dust, I made out flashes of tooth and claw. A yellow dog flung himself from the melee, bloodied from the hip to the toe, and he circled once before diving back in.

Dash's snout reared up to the air, and the big black dog lunged at his neck. I thought for sure my dog were a goner, but he had a trick in him yet, and he rolled away, sending the black dog snapping at the air while Dash twisted back around and bit him on the leg.

The black dog yelped and danced away, and then, meeting my eyes, saw easier prey in me. He darted from the fracas toward where I stood. Dash gave a howl of protest, but three other dogs were on him, and he could no more come to my rescue than I could come to his. I squared my feet and prepared to get hit with the full force of the big black dog smashing into me and biting the life from my own neck.

I clenched my fists. If I was going down, I wasn't going down without a fight.

I saw the bright pink of the dog's gums, the yellowy-white of his teeth, and the cruel fury of his one eye as he cut the distance between us. Foamy slobber splattered from him as he ran. Dash barked and I yelled in answer, and the black dog bounded at me, and then the crack of a rifle tore the air.

The black dog stopped short, startled. The other dogs stopped the fight and looked behind me. Another crack, and they all turned, running away just as fast as they'd come.

I turned to see a white-haired man in a fine gentleman's waistcoat holding a Winchester rifle in the air and striding toward me. Dash hobbled over to me from the other side with a few scrapes on his belly and a bloody cut on his neck, but no injury that looked too serious. He panted as he stood by my side, and as the man approached, his fur bristled once more, ready to defend me if the need arose.

"Good boy," I told him, rubbing the top of his head. "I think this one's a friend." I looked up at the man and addressed him kindly, as it don't do to be short with a man who holds a rifle. "Thank you, sir," I said. "I was in some trouble there.

"It won't do to be out on these streets after sunset," the man told me. "You'll have worse to fear than wild dogs."

"I was fixin' to find the Ward home," I said. "You don't know if they up and left Jackson, do you?"

The man squinted at me. "What business could a boy like you have with them?"

"I come all the way from Lauderdale County looking for a friend of my brother, Julius," I told him.

The man lowered his rifle and smiled. "Julius Burford?"

"Yes, sir," I said, and finally, through all my tribulations, it seemed fortune smiled on me at last.

The man opened his arms wide. "You must be Andrew," he said. "I'm James Ward, Mary's father. I heard what happened in Meridian. Is your family all right?"

"Nobody's hurt, I suppose," I said. "But the house is gone and we're in a spot of trouble."

James Ward frowned, and then he pointed up to a big house with white columns ringing a great portico with a stained-glass rosette set at its peak. "Why don't you come inside and we'll get you something to eat. There's no trouble that a little food and a good night's rest can't improve."

I followed him gratefully. Mr. Ward was kind and hospitable as any good Southerner, and I couldn't rightly square how someone so kind could be for the Union side, when all I'd ever heard about them was their arrogance and tyranny. He didn't seem like a tyrant at all. In fact, he even let Dash come straight inside and eat a fine piece of meat from the finest china dish I ever saw.

CHAPTER 17

A FREE MAN

The dining parlor in the big house was all shiny with polish and dark wood, and we ate off these fancy plates all painted with flowers and birds and such. Dash gave me a look with that floppy-jowled face of his, his eyebrows up, and it was like he knew he wasn't fancy enough to be eating in such a room.

The Wards gave me roast beef and potatoes and cabbage and biscuits so hot and fresh that steam burst out when I split one in half. It felt good to eat hot food and plenty of it, and I drank a tall glass of milk too. I felt full and sleepy before Miss Mary Ward even showed herself.

Mary Ward's father sat at the head of the table, quietly watching me eat, and her mother sat opposite, with me in the middle with the whole dark wood dining table laid out before me bigger than the bed I slept in at home. A colored servant tended to me, and I weren't used to being served so. I knew Mary's father was an abolitionist, which meant he was working to end slavery forever, so the servant must've been a free man, getting paid wages and such. I wasn't sure how to treat him, but Pa always said rudeness were a sign of weakness, and I didn't want to be weak, so I said "please" and "thank you" to the servant, even though I didn't know if it were proper or not.

"You're Julius's brother?" Mary asked as she came into the room on the other side of the table from me.

"Uh-huh," I said. I don't know what I expected, because I'd never seen her before, but I guess I thought she'd be prettier, the way Julius went on about her. She looked like any other girl I'd seen, with long, dark hair and skin pale as bone. She must've spent a lot of time indoors to be so pale. I could see a few lines of her blue veins through her skin, and her thin lips turned down at the edges with her worry.

"You look just like him." She smiled, and that made me feel pretty good. Girls always said Julius was handsome, and I guess that meant I was handsome too. I gave her another look, and I guess, up close, she was prettier than I first thought, sort of like when you look at a moth, how they look all one dull brown color far away, but up close their wings shine and sparkle and run with patterns.

"He wrote me about you," I said. "He wondered why you never wrote him a letter."

Mary glanced at her father, a nervous look that she didn't think I'd notice, but I notice all the looks grown-ups give and think kids won't see. I didn't let on nothing about why I'd come to their house. I had to be careful now. They might have been hospitable to me, but they was still siding with the enemy, and I didn't know if I could trust 'em or not.

"I wanted to." Mary sighed. "But sending letters to a Confederate soldier . . . Oh, how I wish I had!"

Just like that, she broke down crying, burying her head in her hands.

"Now, Mary —" her father scolded, and she ran from the room. This I didn't understand, and my confusion must have showed.

"She is rather emotional," her father explained. "After the siege of Jackson, we have all been quite tense."

"But, sir? What do y'all have to be tense about?" I asked. "I mean, er . . . I thought you sided with the Union. It's the Union that controls the town now."

"Yes, Andrew, but war is a messy business and even victory comes at a great and terrible cost."

"It's just one city. It don't mean the Union's won." He looked at me real hard, and I looked down at my plate. "Sir," I added.

Mr. Ward nodded and frowned, giving consideration to what I said. He didn't yell at me or scold me. He listened to me, and I liked that. It made me want to talk more.

"I mean, Mr. Ward," I sat up straighter and he leaned toward me to listen. "The Confederate States are the ones that got invaded by the North, right? So we're fighting for our homeland, while the Yankees . . . I mean, er, the Northerners, they're fighting just for their government. It's one side fighting for their homes and their way of life and the other just fighting because some generals and the president say they got to. So even if the Union takes all the cities and towns in the South, we won't ever let them win, because then we'd be destroyed altogether. We'll fight to the last man, at least, here in Mississippi."

"To the last man?" Mr. Ward said.

I nodded.

"I see," he rubbed his chin. "And you would fight?"

"I would," I said. "If I got the chance to."

"Because it is your home?"

"Yes, sir," I said. He understood me.

"And yet, Mississippi is my home too," Mr. Ward said. "And I do not, nor have I ever, supported the cause of secession from the Union or the institution of slavery."

"But you don't have to support slavery to support the Confederacy," I told him, just like Pa always said. "We don't have no slaves —"

"Any slaves," Mr. Ward corrected me.

"We don't have any slaves," I said. "But we don't want no outsiders coming in and telling us by law that we *can't* have 'em. We're a free country, after all."

"But are not the black men and women of Mississippi also part of this country? Why should your freedom come at the cost of theirs?"

"Well . . . because . . ." I didn't have no good answer to that. I supposed I couldn't say it was because they liked being slaves, not after I'd seen them running off the first chance they had, not after I'd helped one run. Why would folks put themselves through such dangers, breaking the law and fleeing through hard countryside in the middle of a war, if they was happier being slaves?

I suppose I wanted to say because slavery was just the way it'd always been, but that didn't make no sense neither. Nothing ever stayed the way it'd always been. Things changed. If they didn't, we wouldn't have no inventions or ideas. If they didn't change, then we'd all be like little kids forever, a whole country of little kids, but I weren't a little kid no more, and if I could grow up, maybe so could my country.

But still, I'd always heard abolitionists was bad for forcing their view on us, so that was what I told Mr. Ward. "I guess slavery should end, but it's got to end its own way. No Yankee musket can force it on us. That's why there's so much bloodshed."

"The old ways are hard to change," said Mr. Ward. "It seems to me that force, and only force, will change them. Make no mistake, young Andrew. Change they must and change they have. No matter the outcome of this war, slavery cannot survive. There are more blacks in the state of Mississippi than there are whites, did you know that?"

"No, sir," I said.

"It's the truth. They have tasted freedom, and they will not go back to enslavement. Isn't that right, Joshua?"

"Yes, sir," the servant said, startling me. I'd just about forgotten he was there.

"I purchased Joshua some fifteen years ago," said Mr. Ward. "I gave him his freedom straight away, and then I offered to pay him to stay on and work for me, which, happily for me, he did. Because of this, he's been able to unite his family and build a better life for them. That is the promise of this country, Andrew, and now that all men have tasted its hope, they starve for more of the same. Slavery cannot survive, although I fear much bloodshed is to come before my neighbors reach the same conclusion and reconcile themselves to this new world we live in, one where all men are created equal."

He sounded just like the pacifist preacher, except he weren't no pacifist. He knew it would take more fighting to get his way. He was a smart man, and brave too. Most folks with Union loyalties ran off to the North when the war broke out, but he stayed, just moving his family over to Jackson. I admired him greatly and only wished he was on our side in this war. I couldn't answer his speech, so I objected in the only way I could think to.

"I still don't see why Miss Mary couldn't go writing a letter to my brother," I told Mr. Ward. "It would have done his spirits good and then maybe . . ." I stopped. I'd said too much already.

"Maybe what?" Mr. Ward leaned toward me. I shoved a chunk of biscuit into my mouth to buy a moment to think. I didn't want to let on that Julius had deserted the Confederate Army. Mr. Ward probably would have been glad to hear, and I couldn't bear to see his gladness over my brother's shame.

"Don't pester him, James," Mrs. Ward suddenly said, breaking the silent vigil she'd kept so well at the table. Mr. Ward gave her a stern look, but she did not relent. "The boy has come a long way and has the right to know," she said.

"To know what?" I asked.

"That I'm here," Julius said, bursting into the room with Mary behind him. He looked older than I remembered him when he left, skinnier and with heavy lines on his forehead and a scar on his cheek that hadn't been there before.

I was so stunned to see him in the room that I just sat and stared.

Dash recognized him in an instant. The big dog jumped up on the table, knocking the fine china and the silver and the cut glass bowl of gravy to the floor, where it smashed.

Joshua yelled, Mrs. Ward gasped, and Dash barked, jumping onto Julius, tail a-wagging, and just licked him all over his face. If ever a happier dog existed in all the world, I couldn't imagine it. Dash knocked Julius back through the dining parlor door with his jubilation.

I was still dumbstruck. I expected finding him to be a harder task, but now that I'd found him, I didn't know what to say. He'd been a coward and a sneak and he'd dishonored our family by running off, and now I had to find the right words to say to bring him back.

"I . . . uh . . ." I said, and then I turned to Mr. Ward, and all I could think to say was, "That's why Pa don't let Dash in the house."

CHAPTER 18

TWO BROTHERS, TWO MASTERS

Joshua took to cleaning up after Dash, sweeping up the broken dishes and the spilled food. I tried to apologize, but he just waved me off. Mr. Ward led me to the back of the house, where Julius and Dash were playing in the cool evening grass, rolling about and wrestling.

We watched them from the doorway. The moon was clear and bright, and everything shined in its glow. Watching Dash and Julius play, it was easy to forget all the bad that'd happened and all the bad what was still to come.

Dash would bark and nip at Julius, who then wrapped his arms around the dog and rolled him. Dash would squirm and spring, bounding this way and that, and Julius would laugh and try to catch his tail.

"I haven't seen your brother this happy since he arrived here," Mr. Ward told me.

"How long he been here?" I asked, biting my lower lip.

"The start of October, I suppose," he said. "Over a month ago."

That got me mad at Julius all over again, and no amount of pretty moonlight could make me forget it. All this time when Ma and Pa and me was worried that Julius'd been hurt or killed, my brother'd been living the good life with the rich Ward family.

"I urged him to write your parents," Mr. Ward added, understanding, I suppose, why my face got all crimped and creased and red with anger. "Julius refused. I believe he feels a great deal of shame over his choice to leave the army and also a great deal of revulsion at what occurred during his service. He will not speak it of it — at least, not to me."

I remembered what he wrote in his letter: *I have seen a man along the picket line before the battle so wracked with fear of the advancing blue uniforms across the misty field, that he turned his musket on his self. . . . I saw one boy from our side, a boy no older than you, running in a brave charge ahead, when a chain fired from a Yankee cannon sliced him in half. The poor boy's legs kept running even as the top half of him flopped on the ground like a fish.*

It was a terrible thing to think on, but I'd seen terrible things too, and I was younger than Julius. I seen Winslow shoot a man in cold blood. I seen the hospital and its gruesome healing. I seen our house burned down by Union men. I didn't go hiding out. I was still trying to do what was right and proper. Why should Julius get to hide out when I don't? Why should he get to roll around and play in the grass instead of doing his duty to his state and his family?

I whistled for Dash. The hound dog stopped playing, and his head popped up to look at me. His ears perked.

"Come on over here," I commanded.

Dash looked down at Julius. Then he looked back to me. One of his front paws lifted in the air, like he was on the hunt, which I know meant he was thinking real hard, or at least, hard as a coonhound can think. Even across the yard, I could hear him whine. It don't suit a dog to have two masters, and I guess I was making him choose between us.

Julius looked over at me, his face a question mark. He looked a bit like Dash that way, and I knew I'd done something dumb, putting the dog in the middle of what was rightly a fight between brothers. Dash sniffed the air. Julius

135

patted him on the side and whispered something, and then Dash came running over to me to sit at my heel.

Julius got up off the grass real slow and brushed himself off. He took a deep breath and walked on over to me.

"I'll let you two boys talk," Mr. Ward said, excusing himself and going back inside. The night hummed and chirped with the usual bug business, and I was almost jealous of them bugs. They didn't worry so much as people did. I was jealous of Dash too. He had two masters trying to tell him what to do. Right then, it felt like I had no one but myself.

"Why'd you come out all this way?" Julius asked.

"I come to —" I started, but I wasn't rightly sure how to finish. He waited for me without looking. My words tangled up.

Julius bent down and patted Dash on the head while I stood as dumb as a stalk of wheat, blowing in the breeze. "Ma and Pa okay?"

"They're all right, I suppose. . . ." I said.

"We heard what happened in Meridian," he said. "I thought of comin' back to check up on you, but I worried, what with you helping out the Home Guard, I'd get arrested. Maybe hanged. Or worse."

"That don't make no sense," I told him. "What's worse than getting hanged?"

Julius didn't answer me. He just bit on his lip and his mouth twitched a little, and he got a faraway look on his face, like was staring through a pond, looking at a reflection of the sky and looking at the fish swimming underneath too. A double picture.

"I asked you what was —?" I started, but he cut me off.

"Why'd you come all this way, Andrew? If you figured I was here, you coulda written a letter. When I saw you, I thought something happened to Ma and Pa."

"I said they're all right."

"So then you better tell me why you came after me."

"Why'd you run off? Why'd you leave your regiment and turn deserter?" I felt my face turning red again, my mouth twisting all frowny without my say-so. I was afraid he'd say it was my fault. I know it don't make no sense, but I felt like he could see how I sinned, letting that slave girl get away, and now he'd tell me he knew it and he was punishing me. "Were it my fault?" I asked, and my voice cracked, and just asking was enough to set me crying.

I buried my face in my hands, burning up with shame.

"Hey," Julius rested his hand on my back. He shook his

head and bent down to look at me. "What are you jabbering on about? Your fault? Why should it be your fault?"

I'd carried around all these secrets and now, they just poured out of me with the tears. I told him all about Winslow killin' the deserter and the slave girl I let go, and what I saw at the hospital, and the man stealing Ma's silver, and the abolitionist preacher, and how I didn't know right from wrong anymore, and how him running off was the Lord's way of punishing me for my doubts.

When I finished talking and crying and wiping my face on my sleeve, Julius hugged me close. "Listen here, brother, it ain't no fault of yours. I'm real proud of you, in fact, for what you done. Lettin' that girl go was a good thing, and I woulda done the same in your place, and I reckon Pa would've too."

"That mean we're abolitionists now?" I wondered.

Julius shrugged. "I don't know what's what anymore, Andrew," he told me. "But I know one thing: It ain't your fault I ran off."

"So why did you?" I said. "If it weren't because of me, then I got to know why. You was the one who always talked real big about fighting for Freedom and Liberty and the Great State of Mississippi."

"Maybe it ain't so great as I thought it was before," he said.

"You was never a coward before," I said.

He let go of how he was huggin' me and looked like he was about to toss me in the grass and punch me. I braced myself, but he held his fist clenched and didn't move.

"Running *to* ain't the same as running *away*," he told me, his face hardening against me like a block of granite. "I saw terrible things in battle, Andrew. Things worse than any nightmare. But that ain't why I ran off. I ran off because I'm in love. I'm in love with Miss Mary and no war between the states is gonna come between me and my true love. There aren't enough armies in the world."

He crossed his arms, and I was grateful for that, because he was still bigger'n I was and I didn't want to get laid out by a fist. Not when I had a lot more to say. Talking for me's like letting water out of a dam. Once it starts, there's just no stopping it.

"You ran away, Julius, and we both know it," I told him. "You wrote so in your letter how you was scared. Just 'cause you all mushy-eyed for that Union girl don't mean you get to pretend it's noble that you ran away. Hear that? *Away!* You made a promise to fight for our freedoms, and you made a promise to fight for our state, and you made a promise to fight because Pa's too old and I'm too young, and then you run off on account of a girl? I think that's the worst kinda cowardice and that's why Dash and I come up here, to tell you so! To tell you that you're a coward and a no good brother to me and that you've mixed me up even more than I was mixed up before, and that ain't what an older brother's supposed to do!"

I was crying again already, but the tears were different this time. I didn't feel guilty anymore. I felt mad. Dash whined beside me, and he tucked his tail up under his legs. He didn't like the sound of my shoutin', and to the tell the truth, I didn't like the sound of it much either, but I was going and there was no stoppin' me.

"So you want to stay here and be a coward, that's fine. I'll tell Ma and Pa the kind of son you are." I jabbed my finger up at him. "But I'm not too young anymore, I reckon, and I'm going back to find your regiment and sign up to take your place, and when we march back into Jackson here, you'll be sorry you chose some girl over your own kin!"

I stormed off the porch and marched across the yard, set on walking straight out of Jackson under the cover of darkness and joining up in the war myself.

"Andrew, you can't go off an' —!"

I stopped and turned back to Julius, cutting him off with a look. "Tell Mr. Ward I'm real sorry about the mess Dash made and real grateful for the meal. And tell him I ain't fighting to keep folks like his servant as slaves. I'm fightin' 'cause I'm proud of where I come from, unlike my no-good brother." Then I whistled and waved to my dog. "Come on, Dash," I called him. He hesitated, and I sure hoped he'd come with me this time.

I didn't want to go into war alone.

CHAPTER 19

OFF TO FIGHT

I crept through the silent street, my loyal dog at my side. He snuffled quietly at the ground, and every few minutes he'd stop and his ears would perk, and I'd duck down to hide by a fence or a shrub or the trunk of a gnarly old tree. There was a curfew set and the Union soldiers that controlled Jackson figured anyone out on the street after dark was a Confederate spy and they'd shoot 'em on sight.

They wouldn't be so wrong, neither. I was on my way to join up with the Confederate Army if I could, and I meant to tell them everything I knew about the Union forces in Jackson. I guessed that'd balance out for the spyin' Preacher William'd done. Fair was fair, after all, and one side shouldn't have secrets while the other side had none.

Whatever Dash heard, it weren't no soldiers coming to arrest me, so we kept on. I took a glance back toward the Ward house, but the windows was dark and not a soul stirred. I felt lonesome out there on the road, and I began to think maybe I shouldn't have stormed off like that. I should've at least had Julius write Ma and Pa at Cousin Thomas's to tell 'em I'd gone off to fight for their honor. Someone in the family had to do it, and I wanted them to be proud of me for taking responsibility. As things stood now, they'd worry I'd gone missing when I didn't show up in a few days' time. I'd made a promise to Pa, after all. But I was making up for the promise Julius'd broken. I couldn't figure which promise were more important, and I couldn't keep them both.

I skirted the city, swinging wide the long way, which took most of the evening to get around, but I saw not a soul, citizen or soldier, the whole time. When I got about a mile out of town, I reached a thick hedge. On the other side of the hedge, was this old post fence, and on the other side of that, I saw a whole regiment of men in blue uniforms. I dove down into the dirt and pressed myself flat as I could. Dash lay down beside me, a sign of his good sense and the smart trainin' that Julius had put him through for stalking prey.

The men and their muskets and their officers on horse-back and their big cannons and the fieldworks sat straight between me and the road back to Meridian.

The moon was bright, and that was like a double-edged sword, cuttin' on both sides. I could see almost clear as day, but the soldiers in blue could too, and their lookouts would spot me comin' if I weren't careful. I could keep to the edge of the fence and maybe make it around, careful-like, but I feared my blond head would shine like gold in the moonlight.

I grabbed up some dirt and rubbed it in my hair and on my face so I'd be just another shadow shifting in a shadow-some night. Dash, I figured, could creep well enough beside me, and he sure was a dirty enough dog not to get spotted too easy.

I picked up some more dirt from the ground and rubbed it on the back of my neck. I didn't want to make an easy target if I had to take to runnin' away. The dirt was cold, and it sent a shiver through me as I rubbed it on. I guess the dirt weren't the cause of my shiver, really, but there was no use dawdlin' here. It was time to sneak around if I was gonna find the Confederate lines by sunup.

I took a deep breath and pushed myself up off the ground, and Dash gave out a whine just a moment too late. A hand shot out from the hedge beside me and clamped on my wrist and yanked me right back down to the dirt.

"What'd you smear yourself dirty for?" Julius hissed at me from inside the hedge. He pulled me back, and I slid into the tangle of branches and leaves on my belly. Dash wiggled in after.

"I was trying to disguise myself," I explained, and I did my best to hold down my smile, because after that first fright, I was mighty glad to see him. I didn't know how I was gonna find my way alone. But I didn't want him to know I was glad to see him, because I was still mighty angry at him too. "What're you doin' here? Shouldn't you be back with Miss Mary making mushy faces at her?"

"We do not make mushy faces at each other," Julius grumbled. "You wouldn't understand."

I rolled my eyes.

"Anyway," said Julius. "I can't let my little brother go runnin' off to war. Ma an' Pa would have my head."

"You can't stop me," I said. "Our family needs a hero, and if it ain't gonna be you, it'll be me an' Dash."

"You just a boy," said Julius.

"Am not," I told him. "I talked to a private outta Texas, says a boy my age can be a drummer. And a cavalryman already spoke up about Dash being a fine soldiering dog."

Julius grunted. He held my wrist tight. I tried to yank it away, but he was still stronger than I was, for the time being, anyhow.

"I ain't lettin' you go," he said, pulling at me, and I raised my fist up to punch my brother off me. Dash whined. All his instincts told him to protect his master, but he didn't rightly know which one.

"We make a scuffle, Billy Yank'll come runnin' over, and we're both cooked," I said.

"You don't know what it's like," Julius said, his eyes all red-rimmed. "War ain't glory. It's just some young fools soaked in blood an' anger, trying to kill some other young fools drinkin' up more of the same, all at some rich folks' say-so. It ain't like Pa taught us. There's no heroes, or them that are ain't heroes for some cause of Freedom. They just guys lookin' out for one another, and a cannonball don't care nothin'. Heroes die just as easy as anyone else."

"So you was afraid *then* and you afraid *now*," I said.

Julius swallowed hard. He nodded. "I was afraid for *myself* then. Now, I'm afraid for my brother."

It were one thing just thinkin' Julius was afraid, but to hear him say it out loud, well, it was too much for me. How was I supposed to believe in heroes if even Julius couldn't be one?

"I can't let you go fighting," he told me.

"But I got to," I said.

"You didn't hear me —"

"I heard you fine," I said. "But me and Dash are going, and you'll have to fight us both to stop us."

"You are stubborn as a mule," Julius said, letting my wrist go. I pulled it to my chest and rubbed it.

"And you mean as a snake for grabbin' on me like that," I said.

"Well you ain't goin' alone," Julius said, although it came out like a groan.

"What's that?" I asked.

"I said, you ain't goin' alone," Julius repeated. "Lord forgive me, but I'm comin' with you. Maybe I can talk some sense into the officers if I can't talk none into you."

"But what about —?"

"Don't ask me no questions," said Julius. "If I get to thinkin' too much, I'm sure I'll change my mind, and we ain't got time to argue. Now let's get movin'. . . . We got a long way to go to get around this field and get you cleaned off. No regiment in the whole Confederacy will take on a boy as filthy as you."

I smiled real big as we crept off through a stand of myrtle trees and took the long way round the field, because now I had my dog on one side of me and my big brother on the other and we was on our way to war together. I was giddy with excitement, and I didn't care about none of the naysayers I'd heard: I was gonna prove myself in the heat of battle, and I was gonna show just how heroes still got made in this war.

Too bad I only had half of that right.

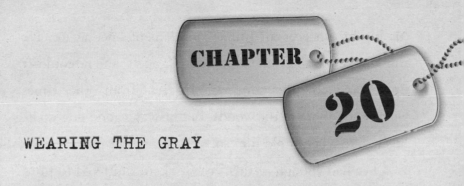

CHAPTER 20

WEARING THE GRAY

"Don't say a word until we pass this Yankee camp," Julius whispered to me. "They got lookouts and sentries, and I even heard of guard dogs that can smell as good as Dash can."

That made me nervous because I was sure we three smelled so powerful bad, even a dog with half Dash's nose could smell us comin'.

We crawled on our bellies past a lookout crouched in a trench on the far side of the fence. Dash growled a low-belly rumble, and we had to hush him up, but even so, the lookout heard it.

"Who's there?" he shouted, and we was close enough to see his musket barrel swaying wildly in the moonlight.

Dash growled again, and I had to clamp my own hand round his snout to get him to hush up. He looked at me with his big brown eyes all full of puzzlement once again. He thought he was *supposed* to growl at strangers, and he couldn't understand how this time was different from other times we'd snuck about in the woods. But he was a good dog, so he hushed up when I told him so.

"I've had enough of this," the lookout muttered to himself and came scramblin' from his hidey-hole, running back toward the main camp of Union soldiers. "They got wolves out there in the forest!" we heard him calling. "I heard a wolf growling at me close enough for spittin'!"

Julius laughed at that, and I rubbed Dash's head.

"That dog's smarter'n us both," said Julius, and we crawled on until my brother figured we'd gone far enough past the camp to stand up and move double-time through the woods.

I let Dash run ahead.

"We can tell any other Union boys we meet that we's just young citizens of Mississippi out huntin' coons," I explained.

"But we got no guns, Andrew," Julius said. "Even a Yank soldier green as springtime'll know we ain't huntin' nothing."

"Well, I guess we better not run into any more Yank soldiers, then," I said. It felt good to trade talk with Julius again, just like we was back home, running through the woods like old times.

We crossed a small creek and Dash jumped and snatched at the water with his snout, sneezing and shaking off so that droplets splattered every which way. We all took a drink from that nice, cool water and kept on in the dark.

"How long you reckon until we find a regiment from our side?" I asked Julius when I saw the first traces of pink from the rising sun in the east. We was climbing a big hill, and my legs ached and my chest burned, and I sure wanted to lie down an' sleep for a bit before the morning came on.

Julius stopped and sniffed the air, just like Dash would do on the hunt. He cocked his head and listened. "I'd say we're just about there."

"Now, how could you —?" I started, but then I got to the top of the rise of that hill and saw starlight stretched out across the valley below, all twinklin' and smoky on the ground. It weren't starlight, but the blazing of a hundred campfires and torches, and with it the murmurings of thousands of men. The white of their tents shone, and the shadows of their big guns stretched as the sun came up on them. In the dimness, we made out the red and blue of the Confederate battle flag flappin' in the breeze.

"You never forget the sound of a military camp readyin' for battle," said Julius. "I'll never forget it as long as I live."

"You think they're readyin' for battle?" I swallowed hard.

"They ain't half a day's march from the Union boys we passed," he said. "You can be sure there's gonna be a battle today."

"Well, then we best get down there," I said, trying to sound braver than I felt at that moment. Julius didn't feel no need to pretend.

"We can just keep on going," he said. "Sneak around like we done before and head on back to Ma and Pa. They'll be worried for both of us."

I had half a mind to say yes to that, to show up at Cousin Thomas's with Julius and Dash, and that'd make me enough of a hero in their eyes, but how could I ever face myself with pride again if I snuck through the night just like a thieving raccoon with stolen scraps? If I was gonna be a hero, I had to go into battle, and I couldn't let Julius talk me out of it, even though I sorely wanted to be talked out of it. I felt like Dash with his two masters, though both of them was me arguin' with myself.

"We got a duty to do before we go home," I said, and I started picking my way down the hill with Dash at my side.

Julius groaned and followed me, and we didn't make it far before a sentry of the army of Tennessee stopped us and demanded our business.

"Private Julius Burford with the Fifth Mississippi Infantry," Julius said. "I got lost a while back and just found my way again."

The sentry looked at him real doubtful.

"This here's my brother, Andrew," he added. "And he come to join up. Now I know he's too young for it, so we best send him on his way."

The sentry laughed at that. "We gettin' ready to face down an army of Yankees, and you want to send a strong boy away? You really did get lost, Private Burford!" He shook his head. "You best go see Sergeant Davis. I'll take you in."

The sentry escorted us down the rest of the way into the camp, and no one took much notice of us walking in, two dirty boys and a dirty dog. The noise of the camp had picked up louder as the fires was snuffed out and soldiers was getting ready to march.

"You there!" a voice called, and we all turned to see an officer on horseback. I recognized him right away as the cavalryman who'd complimented Dash a few days back.

The sentry saluted him, and the officer pointed at me.

"You've come back after all, boy," he said. "I'd know that dog anywhere. I see you picked up another companion and a whole lot of dirt." He laughed at us.

"Yes, sir," I said. "This here's my brother, Julius. . . . The dirt, well . . ."

"The army don't mind dirt, boy!" the cavalry officer said. "You come to join us?"

"Yes, sir," I said, and I heard a low whine that at first I thought was Dash, but then I knew it was Julius.

He stepped up and spoke. "Sir," he said. "My brother here's but twelve years old. I think he's too young to be fightin'. I'm ready to take up arms to fill a place, if he might go on his way home to our Ma an' Pa. They lost their home in Meridian, see?"

"I am *too* old enough to fight!" I yelled. "Uh, sir," I added, and then saluted. Then I blushed because I didn't know what was the proper thing to do. That made the cavalryman laugh again.

"We need drummers. And a dog like that 'un marching out front is sure to strike fear into them Yankee hearts!" The officer whooped. "And you!" He pointed at Julius, who stood rigid. "You look old enough to fight. You got any military experience?"

"I — uh," Julius hesitated. "I fought with 'the Fifth Mississippi at Chickamauga," he said.

"Why ain't you with them now?"

"My service was done," he said, and though it were a lie, I guess it were small one since he was back to fight now.

"Well, welcome back, son! You do your people proud to reenlist!" the officer said. Julius didn't look so proud to get the praise that didn't rightly belong to him, nor to reenlist, but that officer on the horse didn't give him much choice. "Listen here, Corporal," the officer addressed the sentry who was escortin' us. "You take these boys to Sergeant Davis and tell 'em Colonel Jessup says to get 'em outfitted quick. They'll march with us today, and by nightfall they'll be men!"

He whooped and rode off, and the corporal looked at both of us and shrugged. "Come on, *men*."

He motioned us to follow, and before the sun was full risen in the sky, I was standin' there in a gray tattered uniform of the Confederate Army that'd once belonged to another boy. I didn't asked what'd happened to him. I was used to secondhand clothes. Dash sat at my heel and Julius stood before me in a uniform of his own, just about as tattered and worn from someone else's fightin' as mine was. He had a musket and a bayonet and a powder bag, and his eyes was ringed with worry.

"You got what you wanted, Andrew," he said, real sad. "But you gotta make me a promise. When the shootin' starts up, you take Dash and you run. Don't be brave. Just run. No one'll be aiming to hurt you, 'cause even Union folks know what a young'un looks like, but hot lead'll be flyin' every-where, and it don't care how old you are. So you run and I'll find you after, got it?"

"I ain't runnin' no place," I said. "I come to see the ele-phant, and that's what I'm gonna do. You want to run again, you go right ahead. I won't chase you down this time. But you want to come home with your head high, you'll fight too."

"You got no idea what you're sayin', little brother." He shook his head, and some ruddy-cheeked sergeant shouted down at him to form ranks. He stepped up to give me a hug, but I didn't want no hug right then, so we just shook hands.

Then I took my place at the front of the line, and even though I couldn't see 'em, I felt the hot breath and ready excitement of a thousand men lined up behind me. The col-onel on horseback gave me the signal, and I beat my drum with a *rat-tat-tat* to start the march, but I dropped a drumstick and nearly got trampled by the men behind as I bent to pick it up. Dash barked, and that kept a space around me.

I did my best to keep the beat as we marched along the road, so that the soldiers would know the pace, but drumming was harder than it looked. My thoughts raced, trying to remember all the different ways of hittin' the drums that the officers had told me, and what they meant and when to do 'em, but it was a jumble in my thoughts. Dash stayed right by my side, and I was glad to have him there. We was on the way to the fight of our lives, and by the end of the day, nothing was going to be the same.

CHAPTER 21

BLUE AND GRAY

I'd heard the saying "dog tired" before, but never before that morning did I truly understand it. My feet hurt, my legs was sore from marching, and my hand stung from drummin'. Dash stole what sleep he could whenever we stopped, but I was too excited to sleep. I found Julius a ways back in the marching. He was chewing on some hard tack, which I never ate before, and he offered me some.

It was dry and crumbly in my mouth, like the worst biscuit I ever had, and I gave it back to him.

"You remember your promise," he said to me, and I didn't say nothing back because I never made a promise to run away. He just wanted me to.

We marched on into the afternoon. Dappled sunlight lay upon the earth, and the air smelled clean and cool. The colonel told me to stop my drumming, and we marched in silence through the trees, stepping over shrubs and logs and tangled branches.

It was a peaceful day. I listened to birds singing, and I felt almost like I could take a nice nap out there in the woods.

Suddenly, an order came for the march to stop, and I whacked my drum as best I could to tell 'em. The line spread out behind me like a fan opening up as lieutenants and sergeants shouted orders. Men crouched beside trees, their muskets raised into the forest. The birds stopped singing like they knew something was afoot.

Other men, strangers, popped up out of the woods and gave reports of Union forces, then vanished again just as soon as they'd appeared. Scouts and guerillas were like ghosts.

After an age, we heard the first pops of fire from skirmishers somewhere in front of us. The smell of smoke, tangy and tasting of metal, drifted through the woods our way.

"Here we go . . . here we go . . . here we go . . ." a man at my rear mumbled over and over. Men dug little trenches with their feet or picked up stones from the ground and studied them like a stone could tell 'em if it were lucky just by looking at it. I patted Dash just to calm my own nerves. No worry is too great that pettin' a dog's head can't calm it.

We heard a terrible noise coming our way. The colonel shouted the order to forward march, and I banged my drum and we marched straight through the forest onto a smoky field. I couldn't see nothing at first. The field was covered in a thick morning mist, 'cept it weren't morning no more, and the mist was the smoke of cannon fire.

Through the haze, I made out a line of blue across the field, blue hats and blue coats, and then a whistle of artillery fire overhead. It landed in the woods way back, and there was a thundersome noise as it exploded.

"When I give the order to charge," the colonel told me, "you beat that drum just as loud and long as you can, hear me?"

"Yes, sir," I said.

"And once the charge has started, you hang back to help carry the wounded. That's your job, son. Understand me?"

"Yes, sir," I said, wondering if I'd get the chance to fight. Standing across the battlefield with an army at my back, I didn't feel afraid like I thought I would. The fear melted away like river ice in spring. It was replaced by a rush of energy.

I wanted to mix it up with the Yankees that'd brought such misery to my family, turning Julius into a coward and burning our house to cinders and getting my head all confused about right and wrong and good and bad. I wanted revenge. I was, truth be told, excited for it.

Men grunted and coughed. Bayonets clattered into place on the barrels of muskets. Dash panted beside me. At the colonel's signal, I let loose a rolling *rat-tat-tat-tat-tat-tat-tat-tat* on the drums, and behind me I heard the officers shout as one: Charge!

The great swell behind me almost knocked me down. Men yelled and ran, a rush of men with the colonel on horseback in the lead, galloping across the field. The earth around his horse kicked up with explosions of dirt. He just whooped it up loud, waving his hat in the air to rally the men.

The men rushed behind him, screaming as the cannonballs came crashing in. A line of Union soldiers popped up from the ground where they'd been lying in wait. They opened fire with a roar and a puff of smoke. The whole first line of our attack fell. I was glad Julius was farther back in the charge.

I didn't see him through the smoke, but I knew he was out there. All I saw was tongues of fire, like dragons licking the smoke, and soon, gray or blue was impossible to tell. My eyes burned. My mouth was dry, and I sweated rivers. The whole earth shook with the blast of guns and the cries of men gettin' hit. Men fallin' and screamin' out all sound the same, whether they come from North or South, whether they was slave owners or abolitionists, slaves themselves or free men. A cry of pain don't have no politics.

I stood by the trees, where the cannons wheeled up and sent mighty blasts toward the Union lines, and my ears rang. Poor Dash cowered from the noise, and I had to comfort him.

I felt a mighty fool standing back with nothing to do, but just then the colonel emerged from the smoke, riding back toward me. His ear was bleeding where a musket ball had torn the top of it off, but he looked like he was having a good old time.

"The line is breaking!" he shouted back at some of the other officers who hadn't rushed into the fight like he had. He pointed at me. "You feelin' brave today, son?"

"Yes, sir!" I shouted over the din.

"Well, we need you to charge out there and drum the troops. They can't hear my orders, but they'll hear your drummin'. And if they don't, we'll have your dog round 'em up like sheep."

"He ain't a sheepherdin' dog!" I said, but the colonel

didn't hear me, just rode back into the smoke so I had to run to keep up.

I can't rightly say what I was thinking then, or tell all the sights I seen. I ran in and drummed the lines to order, and all the time my eyes burned and my face ran with sweat. I looked out for Julius, but I couldn't see him. I saw other boys just the same age as he was. I saw 'em crouched down and loading muskets with burning fingers as they fired and cussed. I saw others praying and lying on their bellies, covering their heads and hopin' it'd be over soon. And I saw some dead.

Oh, the dead I saw.

Bodies upon bodies, corpses in gray that had been living just an hour ago, lying lifeless on top of corpses in blue that told the same tale. It was a dry day, but the ground was wet and muddy, and the mud seeped red. I stumbled once and fell and came up wet, but it weren't with water. Blood pooled in boot prints and flooded trenches.

"I got one! I saw the Yankee fall," a curly-haired boy with a Carolina twang cried out, waving his musket in the air just as happy as could be, and then his chest tore open where a bayonet popped through from behind.

The blood blossomed around the tip of it, staining his gray shirt the color of roses. The bayonet slid out and he slumped into the dirt. I looked straight into the eyes of a Yankee, no older than me, and his teeth was black with powder, and he sneered and aimed his musket straight at me, and I was a goner for sure, but Dash leaped up and knocked that boy down.

His musket fell away and the boy turned and rolled. Dash's teeth snapped shut around his trousers, but all he came away with was just a scrap of dirty blue cloth. The boy ran, bare-bottomed, back into the blazing battle, and Dash shook the cloth from side to side like he had a prize stick to play with. I ran to the curly-haired soldier on the ground, but he was beyond any help I could give. The Union boy had stabbed him through the heart.

Right then, I hated them Yankee soldiers worse than I ever hated anything in my life, even though I didn't know the curly-haired boy at all. I took my drum off and set it down on the field, and I picked up that musket that the Yankee boy'd let fall. I felt the weight of it, heavier than my hunting rifle and deadlier too. I didn't know fully how to use it, but the boy'd been about to shoot me with it, so I figured

I had one shot loaded already. I was gonna kill a Yankee before the day was out.

I set one knee on the ground and raised the other so my elbow could rest on it and I could hold the musket steadier, just like I'd seen the other soldiers do. I sighted down the barrel into the heart of the smoking battle. I saw men in gray and men in blue struggling fist to fist. I saw others still in lines taking aim and blasting away at each other. Some fell and some didn't. I tried to make out a blue one, but my eyes swirled. I couldn't tell my colors right. I couldn't figure who to shoot. I saw Union men shooting, but I also saw 'em screaming hurt, and crying, and praying, just like ours.

To my eyes, they all started to look just like Julius, and everywhere I turned, every cry of a bleeding soldier I heard, I thought it *was* Julius. These Union men was someone's brother too, wasn't they? They was the enemy, sure, but they was more than that too. They all wanted to live. Who was I to take that right away from them?

Was I a coward? Andrew Burford, who'd come all this way to make his brother join the fight, couldn't shoot when he had the chance!

I started to lower the musket to the ground, and then I saw him.

He was a mean-looking fellow with a thick brown beard and a big scar on his forehead. I recognized him clear as day, even through the smoke and all that'd passed since last I saw him.

He was the soldier that stole Ma's silver when our town was sacked.

Maybe I couldn't shoot no Yankee stranger, just as caught up in this war as all the rest of us was, but sure I could shoot this man, who done my family such a hurtin' wrong.

I raised the barrel again. I squinted down it, taking aim.

Shootin' down a man ain't like shootin' down a raccoon. Men got souls and words, and hopes and all, even bad men like this 'un. I heard tell you should only shoot when you could see the whites of your enemy's eyes, so I looked for the bearded man's eyes.

I don't know who came up with that old saying, 'cause the moment I saw them tired eyes on that Union soldier, I lost my nerve. I saw the face of the man Winslow'd killed back in the lineman's shed, the way he gasped before he died.

I swallowed hard, but I couldn't pull the trigger. I couldn't make my finger end a life. The man with the beard slipped away in a cloud a smoke, and I just knelt there, struck dumb. I felt Dash lick my face, and then, suddenly, he turned away. He barked and snarled, and I saw Julius comin' through the smoke straight at me.

"It's me, Dash!' he shouted, and Dash wagged his tail and *aooo*'d with joy.

"Andrew! Lord, what are you doing?" Julius squatted down beside me. His face was streaked and filthy, and his musket was gone and both his hands was red and bloodied. "It ain't my blood," he said at my questioning looks.

"I —"

"Now put that fool gun down!" He snatched the musket from me. "Why you wanna go killin' for?"

"I couldn't do it," I said. "I couldn't . . ."

"Well, that's the first sensible thing I heard you say," he told me. "I'm glad to you see you're alive. Pa'd have killed me if I didn't get you home. Let's go."

"But the colonel needs me," I objected, but there wasn't much conviction behind it. I wanted Julius to take me out of this battle.

"The colonel's dead," Julius said. "Nearly all the officers. It's a massacre, and we gonna —" A volley of gunfire cut him off, and we ducked our heads low as the lead flew over.

I saw a man's cheek torn open as a musket ball passed through, and when another man's head took a hit, it just popped like a corn kernel in the fire. The blood rained down around us.

"I understand now!" I shouted at Julius. "What you said in your letter! I'm sorry we came back! I ain't no hero!"

"You're hero enough, Andrew," Julius hugged me. "Now come on!"

Just as we stood, a loud whistling sound screeched toward us, and Dash dove back to the ground beneath me, tripping me over, and Julius dove himself on top of me, pressing me and Dash into the dirt.

The shell shrieked, and there was a boom louder than Zeus's thunder, and a flash of white. Something punched me in the head, and the day plunged into darkness and so did I.

CHAPTER 22

LOST CAUSE

"**A**ndrew! Andrew!" I heard my name, like I was being called from real far away. "Wake up, Andrew!"

I opened my eyes, and I saw Dash sitting above me, licking my face. The sun was setting and the red sky looked stained with blood, and the orange light through the distant treetops made it look like the world was burning. My head ached, and my thoughts was a jumble of horrible pictures.

I listened but didn't hear my name no more. It was like I'd heard it in a dream. Dash's big tongue smacked me across the face and licked the dirt off me.

"I'm up," I groaned, pushing myself off the ground. I looked about and saw that I was sitting in a crater made by a mighty explosion. My ears rang as if somebody'd turned my skull into a church bell, and Dash knocked me about with

169

his big, wet nose, trying to get me up. He barked and barked, just like he'd do if we was on the hunt, trying to tree a coon. He ran a circle around me where I sat. Then he ran to the far side of the crater, past mangled bits of cloth and skin that I didn't care to see too closely, and he dug at a mound of dirt. He nosed at it, then he looked back at me with those big, brown dog eyes of his, and he whimpered.

My head was still swirling from the explosion, so I didn't figure what he was on about for a moment, until I saw the hand sticking from the dirt. Dash nuzzled that hand and pawed all around it.

"Julius!" I shouted, and I was over there in a flash, digging and clawing as fast as I could. My hearing started to come back as I dug. There was popping gunfire in the distance. The battle had moved on, and I didn't know who'd won or who'd lost. I heard groans from all around the ground above the crater, but I stayed fixed to my spot, digging.

I got the arm clear of dirt and then I pulled. I pulled with all my strength, and I hauled my brother out from where he'd been buried before his time.

His head hung limp on his neck, and his shirt was all soaked in blood, dried and caked brown now. I ran my hand over him, and felt his back all torn to bits. Seemed like the shreds and patches of his uniform was all that held his body together.

"Julius!" I cried. "Julius, I'm sorry! I didn't mean to make you come back here!"

I wept on him, and I pounded my fists on his chest to wake him, and Dash took to licking and licking and licking his hand, that same spot that'd been stuck out of the dirt. If it hadn't been for Dash's nose, I never woulda knowed to dig there, but I figured we were too late. Julius had dived on top of me, and he'd saved my life and Dash's too, but I feared it had cost him his own.

"You can't die!" I yelled. "Help!" I cried out from down in that crater. "Somebody help my brother!"

Nobody heard me, or at least nobody came to help. The sky was darkening, and I didn't know what to do. I rested my head across my brother's chest, crying into the stinky filth of his uniform. And I felt it move. I felt a rise and fall. I lifted my head and put my ear right up to his mouth, and I felt a tiny breath come out. Julius was breathing! Julius was alive!

"Can you hear me? Julius! It's Andrew!"

Dash barked.

"And Dash!" I added.

Julius stirred a tiny bit, lifting his head just ever so slightly from the ground, and then he let it fall again.

"You okay?" he whispered. His lips was dry and bloody.

"I'm okay," I said. "How about you?"

"Thirsty . . ." he groaned.

"We'll get you water," I said. "Don't you worry."

"I dreamed I saw Mary and she was my bride," he said, and then his body shook, and his eyes rolled back in his head and he spluttered out a cough.

"No!" I yelled. "Not yet! It ain't time for you yet!"

I slapped my brother across the face, and his eyes came back down again and met mine. His hand wrapped itself around my hand and held on. He didn't talk no more. I don't think he could. He just looked at me and held his eyes to mine.

"I don't know what to do," I whimpered. I heard a whooping cheer far off, and then a chorus of voices broke out in song.

"Glory, glory hallelujah! Glory, glory hallelujah!" I'd heard of that song being sung. It was a Yankee song, and if the Yankees were singing, that meant they'd won the battle.

I imagined the whole regiment I'd come with running away through those woods we'd marched in, leaving me and Julius all alone here on the field of battle, without a thought or a care for us. I kept my eyes fixed on my brother, watching him breathe and fearing that every breath he took would be his last.

Suddenly, Dash's ears perked up. His nose sniffed at the air and his whole body tensed.

"What is it, boy?" I whispered. I was afraid that Yankee troops had come back, looking for survivors they could finish off. I'd heard tell that they took no prisoners.

Dash listened, and I tried to hear what he heard, but no human ears are as good as a dog's, and all I could make out was the chorusing of the victorious Union soldiers. Dash must've heard something, though, because he took off. He scampered and bounded up the edge of the crater and ran barking through the battlefield.

"Dash, no!" I called, but it was too late. I heard his barking fade into the distance as he ran away. I ain't never felt more alone than I did right then.

"Come back, Dash," I said, but there was nothing doing. He was gone.

I can't say how long I sat there holding my brother's hand as he strained and struggled to stay in this bleedin' world. It could have been a minute or it could have been a day. The sun finished setting and the night came on, with all the stars above twinkling like they done since the start of creation. I wondered if they saw what horrors went on below, and all the bad that men did to one another because of some silly ideas they got in their heads. Slavery and secession and all them big words I'd heard and said myself . . . what difference did they make when you was lyin' in a crater, holding your dying brother's hand, and your dog gone off, and you didn't have a friend in the world?

I won't lie, I took to a mighty spot of self-pity then, and I sat crying in that crater and begging and pleading with the stars for mercy. Our cause was lost, and there was nothing I could do about it. I was parched, thirstier than I'd ever been in my life, and my mouth tasted of smoke and blood. I wanted so badly to run to the nearest creek and throw myself into its cool waters, but I dared not let go of my brother's hand.

I'd failed to prove myself in battle and I weren't no hero, but I prayed for help that lonesome night, and sometimes, I suppose, even in the darkest nights, prayers find a way of bein' answered. It weren't the stars that answered me, though. It was Dash, coming back barking and howling. He stood proud at the top of that crater, one paw lifted and his back straight. Lookin' up at him, I swear, that dog looked bigger than the whole sky.

And then I saw he weren't alone.

CHAPTER 23

WHAT DASH FOUND

Dash barked again and pointed down at me with his nose. A figure stepped up beside him and cocked his head. It was a boy, about my age, maybe a little taller than I was, but wearing the strap and drum, just like I'd been before I picked up the musket. Only difference was this boy was dressed in the blue uniform of a Union soldier, and he had skin just as dark as the night around him.

"You alive down there?" he said, and his voice was deep and raspy.

"I — I am," I said, my voice crackling like brush burning. That's how it felt to talk, my throat was so dry.

The boy picked his way down the edge of the crater with care not to disturb any of the poor souls whose bodies lay broke and dead around us. He stood in front of me, and seemed to read me like I was a book.

Dash bounded down the crater in two leaps, without half so much care as the boy, and the sight of my dog climbing over corpses made me wince. He came right up to Julius and took to licking his face and nuzzlin' him some more. Julius weren't totally beyond hope because he smiled just a little at the touch of Dash's nose.

"It's you, ain' it?" the boy asked.

I never laid eyes on this boy before in my life. It weren't Alfus. I didn't know no other colored boys, and no Union ones neither, but he seemed to know me and he smiled, friendly-like.

"Who you think I am?" I said.

"Andrew," the boy said, just as sure as can be. "And that'd be Dash." He pointed to my dog.

"How you —?"

I thought I must've died and this was the angel of death. Most strange angel I ever imagined, but I couldn't think of no other way he'd know me. He glanced around real quick, and then peeled off his cap, showin' me his short bristly hair.

"You recognize me now?" he asked, and his voice was higher than before, almost like a girl's voice.

Exactly like a girl's voice.

"Susan," I said, and the boy nodded. It weren't no boy at all, but the very same runaway slave I'd let escape.

"I never forget a dog that's chased me," she said. "When I see him runnin' at me across the field, I thought I'd fallen into a fit, but the sounds of war told me it weren't so. I was awake and that dog'd come to fetch me. He barked and circled and made me follow. I suppose I see why he done so."

I just lay there on the ground, holding on to Julius's hand and looking up at her, trying to believe what my own eyes was telling me.

"That your brother?" she asked.

"I . . . I . . ." I stuttered, because I'd just about lost all my senses. Was I havin' some kind of fit myself?

"He looks just like you," she said. "He in a world of hurtin', I think."

"He saved my life," I said.

"You did me a good turn, Andrew," she said. "So I better do you and your'n the same, if you'll let me. We got a field hospital down the way, and they's got doctors that can heal him up."

I remembered the field hospital that I'd seen, and it made

me mighty scared, but it was better than letting my brother die out here on the ground, so I said yes, that'd be fine.

"You'll have to change from them uniforms you got on," she said. "They don't treat rebels half so well as their own soldiers."

Without another word, Susan started rummaging through the bodies of the fallen men around us, puttin' together Union uniforms for us to wear.

"You gotta change yourself," she said, tossing me a bloody blue jacket. "I'll look to your brother."

She apologized to Julius for the agony he felt, and took to peelin' the clothes from him — all sticky and crusty, they was. He moaned, but she was gentle as could be, bandagin' him up and gettin' him dressed like an injured Yankee. She worked her nursin' on him, and didn't pay me no mind as I changed clothes. I was glad for it. I hadn't never been seen a-changing by a girl, and I didn't mean to start on that battlefield.

Once I was dressed, Susan put her cap on and nodded at me.

"Don't say nothin'," she instructed me. "You talk just like a Johnny Reb."

I thought I talked regular, but I didn't argue. There weren't no time for arguin'. She climbed out of the crater and started shouting for a stretcher. Right away, two more Yankee soldiers showed up.

"That one there is livin'," Susan said. The stretcher bearers, grim-faced and half-dead themselves, climbed down and approached Julius.

Right away, Dash took to barking at them, and the hair on his back went up, and he charged. He didn't want no strangers comin' near my brother. I had to catch him and hold him back with all my might, whispering in his ear to calm him down so that the men could haul Julius outta there.

"It's okay, Dash," I whispered so only he could hear. "They ain't the enemy no more. You done good, boy. You done real good. You saved him, see? You saved me too."

I petted him and petted him, and maybe he understood me and maybe he didn't, but he calmed down, and we followed the stretcher all the way to the field hospital, across the battle-scarred ground, red and bloodied.

Susan stayed with me when we went inside a farmhouse that the Yanks had taken over and turned into their hospital. No one complained about Dash. No one even noticed us, the way adults never noticed us, and for the first time I was glad of it.

Susan stayed with me when the surgeon came around and rolled Julius onto his stomach, and she stayed to help me hold him down as he started screamin' and cryin' because the doctor was pulling bits of metal from his body.

And she stayed with me days after, as Julius started to heal and get his words back, and we learned all about each other. How she'd been born on a plantation and been sold with her mother to the city and then, when her mother got sold away, how she lighted out North to find her. We told Julius how I came along and nearly turned her in.

"You'd've had to lick me in a fight first," she said, and I said I could've, and she and Julius laughed at that, because we all knowed I would have lost, even though she was a girl.

And she told how she found her ma working as a nurse with the Union Army and how she wanted to help too, because she wanted to set all the slaves free, and I couldn't blame her for that. So she signed up for nursin' too, but they had no use for her, so against her ma's wishes, she pretended to be a boy and took to drummin' with this here regiment, through thick and thin and all kinds of battles. She'd seen the Union march cut through the South, and she told us she wasn't sorry to say it, but our side had lost already, though we didn't know it yet.

"I hope so," I whispered, surprising even myself when I said it.

Julius raised his eyebrows at me. He didn't expect such a thing from me neither.

"Like Mr. Ward said, slavery's over and done already, and good riddance to it," I explained. "Girls like Susan don't deserve to be chained up. Nobody does." She nodded and scratched her head beneath her cap, which she still wore, lest any of the others figure out she was a girl.

"And as for all that other stuff . . . well, I seen myself, war don't make men heroes. Some live and some die and some get torn up like you did and some don't. But livin', that makes heroes, and the sooner we can get back to it, the better off we'll all be. Yanks can go back to livin', and here in Mississippi we can go back to livin', and all the slaves can get started livin' as free men, just like everyone'd want to. War ain't livin', and I'd sooner be done with it."

"You sound like a regular preacher," Julius told me, sitting up high in his healin' bed.

"I just wanna go on home to Ma and Pa," I said. "I'm sure they worryin' themselves sick over us."

I looked down at Dash. Susan was stroking his ears, and he was panting every time her small, dark hand pulled the loose skin back from his eyes and let it go again, like a metal spring. His tail thumped the floor. Every few strokes, he'd try to lick her with his big, pink tongue, and she'd pull away and laugh.

"Wanna take Dash out and toss him sticks?" I asked her, and she nodded yes, and the two of them padded out of the farmhouse to play together, while I stayed with my brother.

"You think she was right?" I asked him. "About the war?"

He nodded. "It'll take a lot more blood, I think," he sighed. "But it'll end. What comes next, I don't know . . . except I'm gonna ask Miss Mary to marry me."

He smiled real big, and I smiled too.

"She's just the most beautiful girl in all the —!"

I stood up to cut him off. "I don't wanna hear this mushy stuff," I said. "I'm going out to play with Dash."

Julius laughed at me and let me run off while he stayed back to think up love poems or some nonsense.

I went outside and played with my dog and the girl my dog had found to save us.

AUTHOR'S NOTE

For those Civil War experts reading this book, I must begin with an apology. While the story I've just told is based on the kinds of things that happened in 1863 during the American Civil War, I have rearranged real events to suit my story and made up a lot of other events to make the story better. I will try to make an account of the most egregious examples of where I changed fact to fiction. *Egregious*, by the way, is a word that means "outrageously bad or shocking" — a fitting word for a gruesome war.

On the scale of horrors that brother committed against brother during the Civil War, which raged from 1861 to 1865 and left over six hundred thousand people dead, I hope my factual fiddling is a minor offense.

The town of Meridian, Mississippi, was a major site of Confederate guerilla activity, and in February of 1863, General W. T. Sherman of the Union Army marched in and laid the town to waste. He ordered the looting, burning, and wrecking of every useful structure in the town, from weapons depots and railroad tracks to civilian homes and food stores. When it was over, Sherman is reported to have said, "Meridian, with its depots, storehouses, arsenal, hospitals, offices, hotels, and cantonments, no longer exists." He didn't want anything left behind for his enemies to use.

After the fighting, thousands of slaves did indeed make a run for freedom in the wake of Sherman's army. For Andrew and Dash's story, I moved the destruction of Meridian forward in time a short ways so that it would occur closer to the time of other battles and to the siege of Jackson, but I tried to otherwise remain true to the impact of the event.

There really was a Battle of Chickamauga in late September 1863, and it was a bloody affair, the second deadliest battle of the Civil War (Gettysburg was the deadliest). Chickamauga was a victory for the Confederate Army, and one of the last significant victories they would enjoy. While there were army divisions sent from Mississippi for that battle, I have invented the Fifth Mississippi's role there.

Both the Confederate and Union armies used young boys as drummers, messengers, spies, and, in many cases, soldiers. As the war went on, and recruitment became more difficult, more and more youngsters were compelled to join the fight. At the same time, desertion became a crisis, especially among Confederate ranks. Julius would not have been alone in deserting his post. Far less common would be a soldier returning after a desertion.

As for dogs in the Civil War, they were plentiful on all sides, guarding prisoners, tracking runaways, and carrying messages. In many cases, they did march into battle with the men, and countless hounds and terriers served as mascots for their regiments, lifting the spirits of the soldiers in the ways that only a dog can. I learned a great deal about Civil War dogs from the book *Dogs of War* by Marilyn Seguin (Branden Books).

A few other useful sources that informed the writing of this book were *Hospital Sketches* by Louisa May Alcott (who served as a nurse during the Civil War and later wrote *Little Women*); Bruce Catton's *This Hallowed Ground: A History of the Civil War* (Vintage Books); *The Brothers' War: Civil War Letters to Their Loved Ones from the Blue & Gray*, edited by Annette Tapert (Vintage Books); and *A People's History of the*

Civil War by David Williams (The New Press). Also, I took great inspiration from Stephen Crane's 1895 masterpiece *The Red Badge of Courage*.

Sadly, throughout history, the stories of war are as notable for their tragedies as they are for their heroism. Man and beast alike have died by the millions. In the past, war has often been the only way that leaders can see to solve their problems. The Union victory in the Civil War preserved the United States and ended the great crime of slavery. The fight against Hitler in World War II prevented a murderous regime from conquering half the world and ensured freedom from Nazi rule for the peoples of Europe. And our current war in Afghanistan is being fought for a host of reasons by men of goodwill and great devotion. In all these wars, just or unjust, foolish or wise, dogs have fought and died beside their humans. While dogs will fight bravely beside us, only humans can muster the imagination it takes to make peace.